Alien Savior

The Arathians

Nicole Krizek

Copyright © 2013 Nicole Krizek

Cover art by Aaron Krizek

Photographs from www.shutterstock.com

Edited by Derek McPhee

This book is a work of fiction. Names, characters, places and incidents are either the product of the author's imagination or are used factiously, and any resemblance to actual persons, living or dead, business establishments or locales is entirely coincidental.

All rights reserved.

ISBN-13: 978-1489570994
ISBN-10: 1489570993

DEDICATION

This book is dedicated to my wonderfully supportive husband. Thank you for the brainstorming sessions during dinner, taking the kids so I could focus and for making the wonderful cover art! This book would not exist without you.

I would be remiss if I didn't also thank my parents who have given me nothing but support and encouragement over the years. Thank you to my dad who will probably never read this (which is totally fine!) but always praises my art, and thank you to my mom who also loves romance novels, but will probably blush while reading mine.

CONTENTS

Chapter 1   Page 1

Chapter 2   Page 11

Chapter 3   Page 18

Chapter 4   Page 31

Chapter 5   Page 59

Chapter 6   Page 68

Chapter 7   Page 85

Chapter 8   Page 109

Chapter 9   Page 130

Chapter 10   Page 139

Epilogue   Page 149

CHAPTER 1

Kor hated Vox. He had read the planet's complete description in the ship's database, but all he could think about was that it was hot as hell. And sandy. By the Gods was it sandy. With the way the wind was blowing, he was sure that he'd have sand in places he'd never had sand before. "How much longer will it take to complete the scan?" He asked.

His companion and mate, Ty, replied without looking up from the handheld tablet. "Not long. We just need to scan the rest of the city. I don't want to miss anything." Ty's voice, as usual, was calm and patient. Kor hadn't expected to hear anything different, but he was trying to be hopeful that they'd be able to finish quickly and get off that hunk of sand-covered rock.

Vox was a small planet comprised of deserts and the occasional outcroppings of rock. The majority of the planet was uninhabitable, but due to its remote location on the outskirts of the galaxy it attracted individuals that wanted to stay far away from the law. These thieves, murderers, mercenaries, etc. had built a small city and used it as a trading post for their stolen wares and as a stopping point through space.

Kor was thankful the city was the only populated area on the planet. That meant that by the end of the day, they'd have it scanned and be on their way.

Kor and his crew had been assigned to that sector of space for several months now, having been ordered to search every habited planet, asteroid, or hunk of rock floating in space, to find new species in that part of the galaxy. While they usually traveled in their ship, the Adastra, a science vessel that Kor captained, he hadn't wanted to draw too much attention on a planet like Vox. Instead, he and Ty had landed a small shuttlecraft, and would rendezvous with the Adastra in three days time.

Until Ty finished his work Kor would suffer the planet in silence and be vigilant of their surroundings. The only other things that Vox was known for, besides being able to fry a Frivolian egg with its intense sun, were its lawless inhabitants. The people who lived here adhered to their own rules, none of them good. Kor was not going to allow any harm to come to Ty; the most important job Kor had in the universe was to protect his mate.

While Ty's eyes stayed glued to his tablet, scanning for all life forms within reach, Kor guided him forward. They were currently walking through what passed for a market place in the small city, but Kor was on high alert. He was beginning to hear a ruckus, caused by a large crowd, within a building up ahead. The noise was enough to distract Ty from his scans and he looked up. The closer they got, the more the noise became a roar. Intrigued, they walked into the crude building with packed dirt walls and old fabric, hung to make a ceiling to block out the worst of the sun's powerful rays.

Kor and Ty shared a long look as they realized they had walked into what could only have been a slave auction.

The inside of the building was as dismal as the outside, but it was filled to capacity with the planet's denizens. They had worked themselves into some sort of frenzy. From every corner of the room beings from all over the city were yelling and jostling each another. Some shouted taunts, others sums of money, while others seemed to be yelling just for fun. There was even a group of males on their left, working out their problems with knives and fists.

Slave auctions could get heated when there was someone worth bidding on, but that was rare on planets such as this one which normally dealt in stolen merchandise. Any slave procured legally was sold farther towards the central part of the galaxy where the seller could get much higher sums of money for the slave, especially if the slave was special, or rare in some way.

Kor led the way farther into the room, while keeping a close eye on his mate as they stepped around a group of Grungles. They stood at least two feet taller than Kor's seven-foot height, and were known to have rather brutal character and were quick to temper.

Once the stage was in clear sight Kor stopped, frozen at what he saw: a female, standing on the raised platform at the other end of the room and she was absolutely breathtaking. He was so stunned by the sight of her that it took him a moment to notice that she was shaking with fear, causing the manacles around her wrists to jingle together.

The woman had the palest skin Kor had ever seen, it was nearly pink in color and without scales, horns or fur. She was around five and a half feet tall and scantily clad in a tattered outfit that she obviously had to endure to be sold. He could see she had long brown hair hanging down her back, but Kor unfortunately couldn't see her eyes since she was staring down at the stage.

Kor thought that the Blattarian, a creature that resembled a giant cockroach, was enjoying his role as slaver and auctioneer, far too much. He was currently describing her attributes to the crowd. According to him, she was a female that was strong enough to be used for labor, intelligent enough that she could be taught menial tasks, and that he had generously implanted a Universal Transmitter in her while she was in stasis so she'd be able to understand any of the galaxy's languages. He even pointed out her many orifices to the aliens with tentacles, and that she had plenty of extra pounds and would make a good meal. But to Kor, the most interesting characteristic the Blattarian mentioned was that she was originally from the planet Earth.

Earthers were exceedingly rare out in space because, for the past several thousand years, the Grays had declared Earth under their protection due to its scientific abundance. It was rare to be given the opportunity to objectively observe a developing species and the Grays had been closely monitoring the planet's evolutionary development for several thousand years.

Ty's voice interrupted Kor's thoughts. "Now that's a sight I never expected to see. I never imagined finding a bipedal species in this sector, much less an Earther. A female Earther." Kor could tell that Ty was trying to hide his excitement at finding such an extraordinary creature. He too knew the treasure she could, potentially, be to their species, the Arathians.

Arathians had never been able to test Earther DNA due to of their protected status, but there were no rules against having an Earther in your possession if you managed to buy one off-world. Kor had heard that the Grays' observations had yielded very interesting data, and experiments had been highly successful for the most part. Luckily, Earthers who remembered their experiences with the Grays were often dismissed and considered foolish, or crazy, by others of the species.

Kor forced his eyes away from the Earther and looked at the audience and the Blattarian leading the show. Thankfully slavery had been outlawed on his planet, Arath, for several centuries now, but it was not illegal throughout the galaxy, or even throughout the Galactic Alliance. Kor shook his head sadly. Greed truly was a universal problem. The Blattarian had to be insane to have gone to Earth and violated its protected status, but by the sound of the large sums of money being bid, he would soon be wealthy *and* insane.

"I can't believe they're bidding on her like a piece of meat." Ty didn't bother to hide his disgust. "Look at her, she's trembling in fear."

Kor looked back at Ty and knew that they were in agreement. They couldn't stand by and watch this female be won by any of the creatures assembled when at their hands her future could be worse than death. There was no other choice but to win the auction himself so that he could protect her.

With his most authoritative voice, the one only used when chastising his crew, he shouted: "I bid half a million credits."

The noise in the room quickly dwindled until the sound of his own breathing was loud in his ears. He looked straight at the Blattarian, willing him to decide quickly and close the bidding so they could leave with the little female Earther.

There was no way any creature present could outbid him. Five hundred thousand credits was a fortune, but Kor knew that his government would spare no expense to test the Earther's DNA.

*****

Lacy found herself standing on a small stage in a dirty, hot room, staring, aghast, at the *things* all around her, yelling out sums of money and goods. Money and goods offered in exchanged for *her*. The most disturbing things she heard were all the disgusting commentaries of what the things wanted to do to her, if she became their slave.

She was forced to stand still while the creatures yelled out the foul things they wanted her for: sex, entertainment, service in a home, or a living lawn ornament. One thing, with tusks, even said that it wanted to take her home to be a main course at dinner.

Her body was numb with fear but a small part of her realized that she was just as enthralled as she was repulsed. She looked around the room at the aliens... Aliens! In all shapes and sizes. She had always believed humans were not alone in the universe, but she had imagined that the ETs would look more like the "little gray men" from the science-fiction channel, rather than the six-legged, eight-eyed, scaly, and oozing nastiness that stood around her. And the smell of them all was one of the worst parts. It was a cross between bodies that had gone unwashed their entire lives and rotten trash. The smell was so strong that it made her eyes water and made breathing difficult.

When she had been shoved onto the stage and told to "Stand still!" she had quickly scanned the room looking for a way to escape, but unfortunately the only other way out of the building was a doorway at the far end of the room behind the audience. Even if she somehow made it past all the aliens and out the door, she had nowhere to go. She had manacles around her wrists, barely any clothing on, no money, no transportation, and she had no idea where in the universe she was! All that didn't give a girl too many options.

She gave up thoughts of escape and focused on the creatures surrounding the stage and tried to find the least nasty among them. Sadly, all she saw was various examples of gross, and grosser.

One such revolting creature, stood just in front of the stage, let out a sound almost like a sneeze, and some disgusting globs of green slime flew out of one, of several holes in its face. It nearly landed on her bare feet. When she let out a small cry of shock and revulsion the crowd erupted into laughter and, for whatever reason, the bidding intensified. Apparently they liked her disgust... Nasty perverted aliens.

Suddenly, above all the noise and putridness, a loud, deep voice bid a sum of money, much larger than any of the previous offers. Lacy's eyes followed the turned heads of the crowd and she saw two men who looked nothing like the unclean, fowl creatures crowded around her. They so closely resembled humans that she had a moment's thought: *Maybe she'd been saved!* After she took a longer look at them she realized that those men were not from Earth.

Each stood at least seven feet tall, with smooth caramel-colored skin, black hair, chests twice the width of hers, and the largest arms she'd ever seen. They were wearing matching black clothing that reminded her of a uniform, but were so tight that they did little to hide the muscles underneath. One of them was slightly shorter, but bulkier than the other, and had shoulder-length, wavy, midnight hair that should have made him look soft were it not for the intense glower that he'd aimed at the auctioneer. Clearly he was the one who had bid on her and was waiting to seal the deal. Lacy counted herself lucky that she was not the recipient of the fierce look.

Lacy looked at the male's companion who was standing next to him; he was taller, but leaner, and had hair that was pulled back from his face. He was staring right at her, with a look of displeasure. It made her feel self-conscious of her appearance and Lacy glanced down at herself to see why she should warrant such a look.

She was dressed in the skimpy "clothes" her captor had ordered her to wear. They were comprised of a bra-like top, that exposed more of her breasts than it hid, and a skirt made of long strips of cloth, that opened as she walked, and revealed her skin underneath. She knew that she also had some bruises and small cuts on her arms, legs, and torso, from being manhandled for past two days, and being forced onto the stage against her will. Then, she remembered that her face must also be bruised, from the smacks she had received from her captor whenever she asked a question, or opened her mouth to speak at all.

Overall, Lacy was willing to admit that she didn't look her best, but she was not hideous by any standards. Well, any Earth-based standards, anyway. She had no idea what passed for attractive or ugly out here in the back-woods part of the galaxy, especially when compared to the scaly, hairy, oozing, gross aliens that surrounded her.

Still curious as to what would have caused the man's look of displeasure, Lacy's eyes went back to his. The look of disgust had become one of compassion. In those eyes she saw the sympathy she'd been craving since she woke up to the inescapable nightmare she was in. It was only the fear of being beaten again that forced her to resist the urge to run to him and beg for protection.

She had nicknamed her captor, Rat-Bastard and she turned to look at him as he laughed and demanded proof of such a sum of money. She could have practically imagined the thing clapping his many hands together in glee. One of the two men stepped forward and, after pressing a couple of commands, handed the auctioneer a device that had been attached to his belt. Rat-Bastard looked at the device and asked the crowd if anyone would bid higher. His question was met with grumbles from the audience, so, since no one would outbid the two men, he excitedly exclaimed that she was sold.

Lacy knew she shouldn't, but she felt immediate relief that these men had won her; better them, and whatever they planned to do to her, than the other foul creatures assembled in that place.

The man took the device back from the auctioneer and input some commands. Rat-Bastard's several eyes lit up after being shown the screen and was apparently satisfied because he went across the stage, grabbed ahold of Lacy's arm in an iron grip, and started to drag her towards the men. She couldn't help but let out a whimper of pain as his nasty, claw-like fingers dug into her bicep.

Out of the corner of her eye she saw the leader take one large leap onto the stage, bare his teeth, and growl in Rat-Bastard's face. "Do not touch our Earther again." He said in a calm, but menacing voice.

The bastard immediately dropped her arm and backed away from her, retreating across the stage. Lacy was overwhelmed by the waves of aggression flowing from the male in front of her, who was still staring at Rat-Bastard's retreating form.

Up close, she realized that he was quite handsome. She hadn't noticed the color of his eyes before, but she realized that they were a startling green. She had expected them to be brown, like the darker-skinned people from Earth, but his were a green color that seemed to slightly glow. They were another reminder that these were not mere human men.

She was still standing, her eyes fixed on his face when she heard another voice. "Come here little one." She looked and saw the man with compassionate eyes holding out his arms to her.

Lacy knew that she had no reason to trust those men, but instead of running away, found herself walking quickly to the edge of the stage and allowed him to help her down and cradle her in his arms, against his solid chest. She wrapped her fingers in his uniform just in case he had any ideas of changing his mind about buying her, and planned to give her to the other aliens.

The other male jumped down from the stage, took a long look at her and his companion, and then motioned for them to walk out of the auction house ahead of him. Lacy could hear him walking close behind them as she rode in her savior's arms. She hoped that they were her saviors, and that she wasn't going to be that night's dinner.

CHAPTER 2

Ty could think of nothing else but getting their little Earther to the shuttle and to safety as he navigated the city back to their docking bay. He could hear Kor behind him and knew that his mate was on the alert, constantly scanning their surroundings to ensure their safety.

Finally the docking bay came into view and Ty walked straight to their shuttle's rear hatch. Kor placed his hand on a control panel and the large door opened.

"Ty, go inside and take care of the little Earther. I need another minute here and then I'll get the ship ready to embark." Kor instructed him.

"And where are you going?" Ty asked.

"To finish our mission here as quickly as possible so

we can get off this Godsforsaken hunk of sand and rock."

Ty nodded and carried the precious bundle into the shuttle. Kor closed the door behind Ty and the Earther and walked away.

Ty walked quickly to the Medical Center, which was equipped with the latest in Arathian technology, including a new Medical Unit that was able to scan the entire body to assess injuries and illnesses.

When the doors to the Med Center came into view Ty suddenly felt anxious. He entered and carried the little Earther towards the examination table. After placing her gently on the table he moved to stand up, but was forced to stop.

Her hands were still clutching the material of his flightsuit.

He smiled as he reached down to unlock her fingers from the fabric. It took the Earther a moment to realize what was happening, and she quickly dropped her hands, looking down in embarrassment. Ty couldn't help but smile at the little Earther's reaction. He didn't want her to feel uncomfortable, but he had liked that she had clung to him as if he had been her lifeline.

Arathian males were biologically hard-wired to protect those weaker than themselves, and seeing the little female on that stage, trembling in fear, had undone something inside of him. All he had wanted to do from the moment he had seen her was to take her with them and keep her safe. He wanted to erase that frightened look and replace it with one of bliss.

The instinct had been so powerful that it had nearly overridden his common sense and he had barely managed to keep a tight rein on his self-control.

Ty gave his head a shake to dislodge those thoughts. It didn't help anyone to dwell on the past, and now, with her sitting in the Med Center, he set his mind to what needed to be done to ensure her health.

Ty noticed that the Earther was looking around the room with wide eyes. He made sure his voice sounded calm before saying, "I'm not going to hurt you little one. We won't let anyone hurt you ever again."

She just sat there, silently looking at him, and he wondered if she was trying to decide whether or not to believe him. She must have, because she gave a small nod.

Feeling relieved, Ty turned to grab the laser-cutter to remove her cuffs. She watched him closely, but didn't make any move to stop him when he gathered her wrists in one hand and began cutting off her bindings. He was extremely cautious to avoid marring her soft and delicate skin.

"Thank you." she said once the bindings were off her wrists and had been tossed down the garbage-receptacle so she'd never have to see them again.

With the task completed, he focused on checking her health. He could see the numerous bruises and scrapes on her skin, but he needed the Med Unit to check her for any other type of injury.

"Would you lie down, please?" He tried to keep his voice as non-threatening as possible.

"Why? What are you going to do to me?" Her voice was shaking slightly.

Ty understood her reluctance, but hated the thought of her being afraid of him. It went against his nature to hurt a female, especially since she was hope for his species.

He gave her a small smile and explained, "I want to check you and make sure that the Blattarian that stole you from Earth didn't hurt you on your voyage here. I also want to check if he gave you all the vaccinations necessary for space-travel."

He took a step back and turned away to give her

some privacy as she arranged herself into a laying position on the exam table. He could hear her shifting and tugging on what she was wearing, presumably to cover herself as best as she could. He took a deep breath and tried to will away the arousal he was beginning to feel from thinking of the barely-there outfit. He'd been trying to ignore her attire and knew that he need to find her some other clothing soon... *Immediately isn't soon enough*, he thought.

He hadn't been intimate with a female since he boarded the Adastra and left Arath nine years ago. Females were allowed to serve as crew members aboard ships, of course, or any other job they chose, as Arath didn't have laws limiting females like other planets, but most chose to stay close to their home-world instead of traveling to the far reaches of the galaxy.

Now, in the same room as a very attractive Earther, he couldn't stop his body's reaction. He tried desperately to think of a topic that would distract him.

"Do you remember the trip from Earth?" he asked quickly.

"Yes, the past two days were awful." She replied. "So... are you a doctor?" She asked nervously.

"Yes I am. I'm a geneticist, but I'm also the lead medical officer on our ship, so I'm quite qualified to check your health." He began inputting commands into the Med Unit's control console.

"But, I do have to admit that I've never treated an Earther before. I will make sure to be very thorough before giving you anything."

"Okay."

"Try to lie very still for the next few minutes while the Med Unit is working. It will scan your body and check your health." Ty explained.

Lacy was trying to remain calm and immobile as a large machine lowered out of the ceiling above her and began making a soft whirling noise. Some sort of clear monitors appeared in front of the doctor and began throwing up data… Lots of data.

She tried to look, while not turning her head and she caught glimpses of must have been an alien language. She didn't understand the language, but she recognized the images of her body as it was being scanned. The doctor scrolled through what seemed like an endless amount of information.

After a while the machine overhead stopped its low hum and retracted back into the ceiling. She felt vulnerable, laying on the table, so she sat up and tried to be patient while he studied the scans. She couldn't stay quiet for long with the hundreds of questions that whirled around her brain.

"So, you mentioned vaccines earlier. Did that bastard give me any?" She suddenly blurted, louder than she had wanted to be.

He chuckled at her outburst but said nothing for a moment longer. After double-checking her scans, he replied while barely masking his disgust. "No, I do not see any of the protein structures in your system."

Lacy sat, shocked at what she had just heard. It only took a moment for her shock to turn into anger.

"You mean that asshole stole me from Earth, brought me through space to a nasty-ass planet, full of nasty-ass aliens, and if that wasn't enough, he didn't think his investment important enough to keep healthy?" Her voice was little more than a shriek by the end. The doctor looked at her and it appeared like he was in full agreement.

"But you're here now, and I'm going to take care of you."

Heaven help her, but she believed him. She knew

that he'd do everything to keep her safe, though she didn't know why. Her anger dissipated and she suddenly slumped forward, her face in her hands. The exhaustion that she'd been keeping at bay for days had found her.

She heard him take a few steps away from the monitors and come towards her. "It will take me a while to go through all this data. Would you like to get some rest until I'm finished? I tend to get engrossed in my work so there's no reason for you to wait here."

"Yes." She said with real relief. Sleep sounded divine after the horrifying experience of the last few days. "I'd love to get some sleep."

He held out his hands to help her down from the examination table. Lacy watched him for a couple of heartbeats before holding out her hands.

Instead of taking her hands he reached forward and picked her up by the waist, gently lifting her off the table. He removed his hands after a moment of holding her in front of him, but then took her right hand in his left and guided her to the door, as if he couldn't bear to sever physical contact.

The doctor led her down halls, all painted in varying shades of boring gray, past several doors, until he stopped at one in particular. He opened the door and led her inside, allowing her to examine the sparse décor. She found a large bed and an adjoining door, but that was all there was. There were no personal touches at all.

"You can sleep here for as long as you wish." He said, stepping away from her and opening a closet. He picked out some clothes and held them out to her. "Anything I give you will be too big but, I'm sure you'd like to change out of that… those… clothes."

"Yes, I'd love to change," she said with enthusiasm while taking the offered clothing. "Do you also have a place for me to wash up?" she asked hopefully.

He pressed his right hand on another panel, opening

a door that led into a smaller room. She looked inside and saw vaguely familiar things: something that looked like a toilet and a stall with a touch panel. There was no shower-head. He walked in after her and showed her how to use, what he called, the cleansing stall. After they stepped back out into the main room he surprised her by bowing deeply.

"I will leave you to rest now little one." he said. Then he left her alone in the room.

She took a moment to stare at the bed. It was huge, the biggest she'd ever seen. "I know they're big boys but sheesh! This bed is as big as my entire bedroom back home. He must like to sprawl." she muttered as she walked into the bathroom, still carrying the clothes she'd been given.

She felt no remorse as she removed the garments she'd been forced to wear, and took delight in kicking them into a corner of the room. She promised herself that she'd burn them as soon as she could. After stepping into the cleansing stall, and fumbling with the controls a bit, she was delightfully clean and wearing clean clothes.

She felt like it was getting harder to stay awake. It was almost as if the bed was calling to her and she gave in eagerly, crawling under the blankets in the center. As she put her head down on the pillow, she caught a wonderful scent and she found it comforting. She dimly registered a second scent on the sheets, but she drifted off before the thought could take hold.

CHAPTER 3

Ty had to keep himself from sprinting back to the ship's Medical Center after he closed the door to his, and Kor's, bedroom behind him. Just in the small amount of information that he had been able to review, he had already determined that, not only were Earthers much closer cousins to his race than previously thought, but that they were the greatest chance for the salvation of his race. He was more than eager to dive into her DNA and the mysteries of her body.

In more ways than one.

He thought about her sleeping in their bed and found that he was very pleased with the thought. He had considered taking her to one of the guest quarters to sleep but couldn't stand the idea of her sleeping anywhere else but in their bed. He wanted her scent on their sheets and he wanted her to snuggle into their pillows and blankets to find peace and rest.

His mind drifted to thoughts of her pale skin and wondered if she'd be that color all over, or if her core was a darker shade of pink. He immediately felt blood rush to his cock and had to force himself to focus on the scans on the screens. There was a chance that she was the key they'd been searching the galaxy for, and his race couldn't wait around while he had erotic fantasies about the softest skin he'd ever touched.

*****

Not long later, Kor got back to the shuttle and worked quickly to depart. The shuttle departed the space-port and followed the course that would rendezvous with the Adastra.

He'd had some worries about leaving his ship in the hands of his second-in-command, Simdon, but the male was eager to prove himself and Kor needed to give him his chance. Now, another challenge had presented itself. The little Earther that he and Ty had purchased.

It was estimated that the Arathians had about another 100 years before they went extinct. Unless, of course, they were successful in their hunt for a compatible species. Since no one was allowed to interact with Earthers on their planet, they had never been tested for compatibility. In a way, Kor and Ty had been very fortunate that there were no rules against buying them from auctions on other planets.

And the money he had spent? She had been very expensive, but the government would almost certainly support his decision to take advantage of the opportunity.

Potential extinction was not the only reason he hadn't hesitated to buy the Earther. There had been something about her standing on that stage, looking more frightened than any female he'd ever seen, that had driven him. Something deep inside of him had rebelled at the very thought of her fear. The truth was that he would have paid double what he had to take her away from there, and he knew that Ty would have agreed.

As the shuttle left Vox's atmosphere, Kor thought about the three-day journey to meet the Adastra. It was plenty of time for Ty to go over her scans. He thought about how lucky he was to have such an esteemed mate as Ty.

Ty was the leader in the field of Arathian genetics, and together they had been traveling through the galaxy testing every species they could find to discover a solution that would save their race. He couldn't even imagine what his life would be like without the easygoing male. The years of being mates had been the happiest of his life, but he couldn't help but feel like there was something missing in their lives. He had thought it was because they had spent so much time away from their home-world, but he was beginning to think it was something else.

He had a sudden urge to see his mate.

Kor quickly walked to the Medical Center and found Ty engrossed with whatever was on the vid-screen in front of him. Data flashed by and Ty seemed to be processing everything as quickly as he could.

Ty spoke without looking up. "Did you come to see if I had results? I only scanned her a few minutes ago and haven't been able to go over everything yet."

"Actually I came to see you," Kor said as he moved to stand against Ty's back and bring his arms around Ty's chest to bring them closer together.

Ty stilled for a moment but Kor knew that as much as Ty was dedicated to his work, he could never say no to his mate.

"You came to see me? Did you bring me something? Maybe a present?" Ty asked as he pressed the firm swells of his ass against Kor's erection, causing it to ride his crease.

All Kor managed was a grunt before Ty spun around

in his hold and pressed their mouths together in a demanding kiss. Kor took over the kiss by lacing his fingers through Ty's long hair to hold him still as he began sucking on Ty's tongue. He was imagining doing the same thing to his mate's cock. He loved Ty's cock. He loved taking it down his throat, and the sounds his mate made when he rubbed his tongue along the vein on the underside before sucking him to the back of his throat.

It was always like this between them, a need for one another that shred all hints of self-control and turned them into primal animals.

Ty must have been able to read his thoughts because he groaned, low in his throat, and began rubbing his cock against Kor's. There was nothing hesitant about the move, there was nothing but need.

Kor broke off the kiss to nuzzle the side of Ty's neck where he smelled the strongest. He kissed and nipped while unzipping the front of Ty's flightsuit to reveal his sculpted torso.

Kor dug his hands under the material, trying to touch him everywhere at once while Ty struggled to get his arms free from his sleeves. Once Ty was able to, he started tearing at the closure of Kor's suit muttering, "Off. Off. I want it off." Then growling, "Get it off, Kor!"

He was taking too long.

Kor chuckled as he stopped touching Ty long enough to get his own flightsuit off, finally freeing his own cock, which he could swear was hard as steel. The second it was free, Ty was on his knees and had sucked Kor's length down his throat before Kor could support himself with something. He quickly grabbed ahold of the Med Unit's table as Ty hummed along his length, sliding his mouth back up to the tip.

"Fucking hell Ty, are you trying to kill me?" Kor

demanded, practically cross-eyed.

Kor looked down and saw a twinkle in Ty's eyes, right before he closed them and dropped his mouth back down Kor's cock until his nose rubbed against Kor's pelvis. Up and down he went, before adding a hand to Kor's balls, rubbing them roughly just as he knew Kor liked.

When Kor really started to pant, Ty broke off his attentions with his mouth. He wrapped his fingers around Kor's shaft and kept stroking as he said, "Imagine what it will be like when we get her in bed, naked, and spread for our pleasure."

"Ty! Shut up or I'm going to blow all over you," Kor said frantically. Ty knew that Kor loved to talk dirty during sex, and he knew just how to rev him just right.

"What do you think she'll be like? My scans tell me nothing about her color or taste." Ty continued showing no mercy. "Do you think her nipples will be brown like our skin, or a sweet pink? I can't get my mind off them."

Ty kept stroking with one hand while the hand on Kor's balls traveled back, and started a barely-there touch, right behind his sack, nearly driving Kor insane.

"Do you think she'll take us in her mouth? I hope she will. Imagine how good she'll feel."

"Ty!" Kor didn't know if he was asking for more or for him to shut up, but he was nearly there with that perfect pressure and the picture Ty's words had created in his mind.

"Close your eyes and imagine she's doing this to you." Ty caught Kor's cock in his mouth again and sucked him down to the base while rubbing Kor's sweet spot, behind his balls, with the other hand.

Kor didn't stand a chance, not with Ty going down on him like he was and the image of the naked Earther in his head. He tensed for a second then roared his release down Ty's throat. Ty took him deep and sucked every drop out of Kor's cock before releasing it. He gave it a few last licks before nuzzling and kissing Kor's groin and hips, and looking up into Kor's eyes.

By the Gods, Kor loved his male. As furious as their lovemaking always began, it always ended with them in each other's arms, cherishing one another. But the lovemaking was not over yet.

Kor bent to grab Ty under his arms and yanked him to his feet before fusing their mouths together in a gentle kiss that quickly heated. Kor could feel Ty's hard cock pulsing between their bodies so he reached down and wrapped his fingers around it.

Ty gasped and began kissing Kor frantically. Clearly he had little control after talking about the Earther.

Kor used Ty's natural lubrication to stroke him firmly until Ty's hips were swinging uncontrollably to meet his downward strokes. Then Kor backed off, slowing the pace and easing on the pressure. Ty let out a groan of frustration and let his head drop forward on to Kor's shoulder.

"You've been thinking about the color of her nipples, but I've been thinking about her sex." Kor said in Ty's ear. "What do you think it looks like, wet and glistening with her juices? What will she taste like? I can't wait to see her naked and spread out on our bed, waiting for us to taste every inch of her creamy skin, like a perfect dessert."

Ty gasped, obviously liking Kor's words.

Kor decided they'd both had enough of the torment and tightened his grip on his mate's hard cock, stroking and rotating his wrist at his head.

Ty tightened his arms around Kor's shoulders and when his breaths became moans Kor caught Ty's shoulder with his teeth, unable to stop the show of possession, as Ty's warmth shot all over his hand and their stomachs.

They stood there for a while, catching their breath, and supporting each other. Finally Ty lifted his head to gently kiss Kor. He smiled then stepped away to grab cleansing rags. He cleaned both of their torsos and Kor's hand. Neither talked about the fact that the Earther had obviously slipped into their minds quickly, and neither seemed troubled with the result.

*****

Lacy emerged from sleep slowly and opened her eyes. She stretched languidly on the bed as she was greeted with darkness. *This is not my room*, she thought.

Her memories came flooding back to her as she sat up in the bed: being abducted right out of her car, waking up in a nasty cell to laughing evil aliens, being slapped, and yanked by the hair to a stage where she was sold.

Then she remembered dark men, taking her to safety. The doctor had said that she was safe and she had believed him, now she was having doubts. What did she really know about these men? How were they going to treat her?

Before she could think herself into panic the door to the room whisked open and in walked the doctor with the other man. One of them turned on the lights.

Holy mother of muscles she thought. They both looked good enough to eat in their form-fitting, long sleeved shirts and snug pants that left little to the imagination. And damn that imagination for conjuring up images of how much better they would look without the uniforms. She had to give her head a little shake to get her mind back on track and look them in the eyes.

"Good morning little one." the doctor said with a large smile. "How did you sleep?"

"Like a log!" she replied, without thinking. At their questioning looks, she amended herself. "I slept very well, thank you." She gave him a small smile in return. She made a mental note to keep human colloquial terms to a minimum. Apparently the space-translator-thingy that was implanted in her ear had its limits.

"We realized last night that we haven't been properly introduced. My name is Tyrelian dan Menes and this," he held out his hand to indicate his companion, "is Captain Kor'ijak dan Rubis, captain of the science ship the Adastra."

"It is a pleasure to meet you." Kor said while giving her a formal bow, which made her feel strange since she was sitting up in bed clutching the sheets to her chest, and wearing Tyrelian's shirt as a nightgown. "Please, call us Ty and Kor." he said once he straightened. "May I ask your name?"

"Lacy Woods."

"It's a pleasure to meet you Lacywoods." Kor said with a smile.

"Just Lacy is fine." she said shyly, and a little amused by his confusion. "It's nice to meet you too." It sounded a bit thin, so she added, "I can't thank you enough for what you both did for me yesterday." She faltered. She wanted to add more but couldn't find the right words to convey her feelings.

The men seemed to ascertain her thoughts because they both smiled broadly. "You're very welcome. Now that you've had a chance to rest would you like something to eat?" Kor asked.

To her horror, the mention of food caused her stomach let out a huge rumble and Ty chuckled. "I'll take that as a yes."

Shyly, she smiled back at them and moved to get out of the bed. They both stepped forward and held a hand out to assist her. After a moment's hesitation she accepted and allowed the men to help her in climbing out of the huge bed.

Once she was standing she remembered that she wasn't wearing any bottoms. Even though the shirt she wore nearly touched her knees, she felt a blush creep over her cheeks as she tried to tug the shirt down further.

Kor noticed what she was doing and smiled at her. "Why don't I get you something else to wear?" He brought his hand from around his back to reveal a bundle of fabric.

She didn't realize what it was at first because she was busy looking at the color. It was a beautiful and rich blue. One of her favorite colors. "It's beautiful…" she said in wonder.

He let some of the material drop and she saw that it was a dress. One of the most masculine men she'd ever seen was holding up a delicate dress, which he had obviously bought for her, and looking at her expectantly.

"I hope this wasn't also in Ty's closet…" she said with a nervous smile.

Kor gave a small chuckle. "No, I bought this for you back in town, before we left. I thought you might like something wear, other than that costume you had on."

She didn't know what to say.

Kor mistook her silence for displeasure. "If you don't like the color we can find you a new one at the next port, but I heard that Earth has many oceans, so I thought you might like the color blue to remind you of your homeworld."

She gently took it from him and stroked the material, still smiling. "Thank you Kor, I absolutely love it." She was feeling overwhelmed as she went to the bathing chamber to change.

From behind her, she heard Ty say to Kor: "You've

never bought me clothes." There was humor in his voice.

It only took her a moment to change into the simple, but beautiful, blue dress and then rejoin the men. She was met with wide eyes from them both that made her slightly self-conscious. She looked down to make sure she had it on right, then finally had to ask, "Do you like it?" to break the silence.

Ty found his voice first. "You look beautiful." His sincerity was evident.

After hesitating a moment she took his offered hand and smiled brightly. Ty led her out of the room into the hall, Kor following closely on their heels.

Lacy was led through the ship by the hand towards a heavenly smell. What had to be a kitchen came into view and she was surprised to see several plates of food, already out on a large table.

"Don't worry, Ty is a wonderful cook." Kor said from her side.

"Although, I'm afraid that I don't know any Earth dishes, so this will all be foreign to you." Ty said as he motioned for them to all sit down on a long padded bench on one side of the table. It reminded her, in a way, of an over-sized booth at a restaurant. She slid in with Ty at her left and Kor sitting her on her right.

"That's ok. When in Rome…" she responded. She gave a small laugh at the men's obvious confusion. Thankfully, she was saved from having to explain by her stomach letting out another loud rumble.

"Shall we eat now?" Ty asked.

"Yes please!" she replied eagerly.

Lacy tried not to think about how nice if felt to have the solid presence of the two men at either side of her, instead she looked at the plates of food on the table. It reminded her of what she would call "family style" eating, but without smaller plates to serve onto. Before she could ask how to proceed, Kor grabbed a bite-sized morsel with his fingers and slowly brought it to her lips.

"Here, try this. It's Frivolian meat."

She was afraid to ask what a Frivolian was, and thought it better to remain ignorant as he popped the piece into her mouth. It was warm, delicious, and seemed to melt as she chewed. It felt like she hadn't eaten in ages and thankfully, between Kor and Ty, they kept the pieces coming and didn't allow her to grab anything herself.

Finally she had to push herself away from the food. "I can't eat another bite!" Only then did they eat.

She sat and thought that it was odd that they fed her with their fingers and only once she'd had her fill did they eat. These men were certainly an enigma.

Once they had cleaned the plates, she gathered her courage. "So… What are you guys? I mean, I know your names, but you're not human… right?" The question made them both pause, probably to gather their thoughts. She'd been silent for so long that her question must have been a surprise.

After a moment, Kor finally replied. "We are on a mission for our planet, Arath. I am the captain of the Adastra, a science ship. Ty is the chief geneticist on our planet."

Wow, so the guys were important on their world, she thought. "What are you going to do with me?" she asked.

"We will take you back to our ship and keep you safe." Ty said, without hesitation.

Being kept safe sounded like a good plan, but what she really wanted was to go home, and to pretend that the last few days had never happened. Maybe hire a really good shrink to help her convince herself that this had all been an elaborate dream. Brought on by exhaustion. Or something.

"Won't I be less of a bother if I'm back on Earth? Why don't you just take me home?" she asked.

The men shared a glance then Kor slowly explained, "We cannot, little Lacy. The Galactic Council has decreed that any Earthers found off-world are not allowed to be taken back to Earth. The council is worried that they will tell other Earthers about what they have seen and influence the natural progression of your world. Even if it were allowed, Earth is very far from here and, unfortunately, we can't spare the time to take you there."

Lacy felt her heart begin to race. Who the hell was the Galactic Council and how dare they decree anything to do with Earth? "But we can't be that far from Earth!" Lacy said, starting to panic, "Why don't you secretly take me back? I promise I won't tell anyone what's happened to me." She looked back and forth, between the men, and saw twin expressions of sadness.

It was Kor that spoke first. "We are farther from Earth than you think, Lacy. Even aboard the Adastra it would take us nine months just to reach Earth."

Lacy was stunned. "Nine months! How is that possible? I was only on that Bastard's ship for about two days!"

Ty could see Lacy's panic rising and started rubbing her back soothingly. When she turned to him he saw the tears gathering in her lashes. He wanted to break down and promise her anything to get that look of utter sorrow out of her eyes. "I'm so sorry, little Lacy. I could tell from your medical scans that the Blattarian put you into a cryochamber while you were transported. For you it would have seemed like you had just fallen asleep, while in reality months went by, perhaps longer."

"I'll never go home then." She sat quietly, staring at

the table, and Ty could tell that she was trying to process what he had told her.

"I'm sorry." Ty could see her crumble before his eyes and a part of his heart broke right alongside hers as she began crying into her hands.

He gathered her onto his lap and she buried her face into his chest, quickly soaking his shirt with her uncontrolled tears. He held her to him tightly while Kor watched, sadly, from nearby.

*****

Lacy felt as if she was falling apart, piece by piece. In a moment she had lost everything in her life. She had lost her family, her friends, her home, her possessions, even her job. Thinking about her family had her crying even harder. She would spend the rest of her life not knowing how they were, or if they were happy. Had one of them adopted her cat when they realized she was missing?

After a time, her sobs turned into seizing catches of breath in her chest and her tears stopped flowing. The men quietly sat with her, while she tried to accept that she would never again return to Earth.

She had always been the type of person that tried to not dwell on the past, instead looking forward. Those two men were her future and she didn't know if that was a bad or good thing. She decided that she'd rather know what they intended to do with her than make assumptions.

"Why did you buy me?"

CHAPTER 4

Ty didn't know if now was the right time to tell her about Arath's problems, but when she sat up and looked at him, her large blue eyes still damp from tears, he knew she deserved to know the whole truth. "The simple answer is that we bought you to protect you. Honestly, though, it's much more complicated than that." Ty said.

"I want to hear it all." she said, determined to know.

Ty reluctantly set her down and stood up. He always had to move around when he was having a heavy conversation so he would need to be able to pace. Lost in thought, he barely noticed that Kor had shifted Lacy into his own arms and they were both watching him.

Ty took a deep breath and began. "I have to begin with a little history lesson for you to understand. Our race has a long history of violence and war. We are known throughout the galaxy as warriors, and for a time our advancements were mostly in the fields of defense and weaponry. A couple of generations ago we achieved peace in our quadrant and, thus, began other pursuits."

Ty left out parts of his people's history, he didn't

think Lacy needed to hear about how aggressive his race could be while he and Kor were trying to gain her trust.

"We reached an age of enlightenment, and during that time there were great advances in technology and medicine. Both fields that were believed to be of great benefit to the people. Even with our medical advances, there had always been diseases within our race, passed down through genes. A generation ago the Arathian Council decided that medical efforts were to be focused on the elimination of all genetic illnesses. A vaccine was created to do this and it had a wonderfully high success rate. It was administered to everyone on the planet within a year. Sadly, in their haste to help the species, they doomed us all."

Ty stopped for a moment as he thought of the day he had been given the vaccine, and how happy his parents had been that their son would not die from the hereditary disease that had killed his grandfather. It had been a day of joy.

Tragedy followed soon after.

He shook his head and continued, "The doctors hadn't had time to properly test the vaccine for long-term side effects. After it had been distributed throughout Arath, it only took a year before we realized that we were no longer able to procreate." He glanced at Lacy when he heard her gasp, but forced himself to continue.

"The vaccine fundamentally changed our DNA and made it impossible for us to reproduce. So far, we haven't been able to correct the problem. We have scientists back home trying to find a solution, but we also sent out science ships, like the Adastra, to seek help elsewhere."

"What do you hope to find?" She asked quietly.

"There's a legend on our planet, that we were created by another race, long ago. It was said that the race seeded many other planets in the galaxy. We hoped that if we found another such species, that our DNA would be close enough that we could somehow use it to save Arath."

Kor finally spoke, "We have been searching for several years without success and we were beginning to lose all hope. Until we saw you."

Lacy turned to look at him. "I don't understand."

"Think about all the aliens you've seen so far, and how diverse they are. Now, think about how similar we look to you." Kor explained, "Ty and I don't think its coincidence. We think Earthers, like you, may be our distant cousins, so to speak. The hope for our species' future."

She looked at him, her eyes wide, then finally said, "Ok, let me get this straight. You think Arathians and Humans... Earthers, might have both been created from this master race, which is why we look so alike, and you want to use my DNA so you can reproduce?"

Ty came closer to sit on the table near Kor. "If your DNA is compatible, we want to use it to fix the problems we have with our own DNA, which, as a result, should fix our reproductive problems."

"You've both been given the vaccine, I'm guessing?"

The men shared a sad look before Kor answered, "Yes, we were both given the vaccine. I was thirty-two years old when it was administered throughout Arath."

Lacy looked to Ty but his response was slower. "I was given the vaccine when I was twenty nine, and Arath realized the side effect shortly after. That was twelve years ago."

Lacy thought that Ty was finished on the subject of his vaccination, but he surprised her by taking her hands in his own and continuing.

"I, along with our world, was incredibly disappointed when we found out about the reproduction problems.

You see, I've always wanted children. It was my goal to find mates that I would love, and build a family together. Once we found out that the vaccine had made us all sterile... I was devastated. It's what prompted me to focus on genetics and join in the hunt for a cure. I want it as much for myself as I want it for the rest of my race."

Lacy sat quietly trying to process everything the men had just told her. Ty seemed so sad when he talked about what happened to his race, and wanting children, and she couldn't help but feel empathy for those men who had dedicated their lives to saving their species. She realized that she wanted to help them in any way that she could.

Really, it was an easy decision.

She could either help them and their entire race by offering up some of her DNA for study, or say no and possibly condemn an entire race of beings to extinction. The thought of the latter made her nauseous.

With her mind made up, she looked Ty in the eye and asked, "What can I do to help?"

"You mean you'll help us?" Kor asked.

The poor man was afraid to hope. It reinforced her resolve. "Yes. I want to help you, you and your world, if I can."

Kor suddenly grabbed her from behind and crushed her to his chest in a massive hug. "Thank you." he whispered. She looked at Ty's smiling face for a moment before he also caught her in an embrace. The moment he released her, he asked, "Can we start now?"

Lacy thought that he looked like an excited child and she couldn't help but let out a little laugh. When she nodded, she was once again scooped into Ty's arms, away from Kor, as he practically ran to the Medical Center.

*****

"So…how are you going to extract my DNA?" Lacy asked as she once again found herself sitting on the table in the Medical Center. Her overactive imagination was going crazy, trying to picture what kind of sample he was going to take. Were the stories of alien probing true? Was he going to probe her *now*?

Actually, there was one kind of probing that she wasn't against trying. Just the thought of the bulges in Ty and Kor's pants caused her cheeks to heat in a blush and her pussy to start throbbing. It had been a long time since she'd had a good probing, *any* probing actually, even if she ignored the months in stasis.

The last time had been nearly six months before her kidnapping, and it wasn't anything worth remembering. The man had fumbled through the motions and she had faked it to get it over with. Her instincts told her that wouldn't be necessary with Ty or Kor. They probably had great probes that were proportional with the bulges of their muscles, clearly defined by their tight-fitting flightsuits.

When she looked up she saw Ty looking at her expectantly, and she realized that he had been talking to her. Lacy shook herself out of her mental vacation and told her libido to cool down. "I'm sorry, what did you say?"

He smiled at her patiently, then repeated, "I said that I only have to take a blood sample from you. It will be quick and painless, I promise. Would you mind laying down and giving me your arm?"

"Oh… Okay." She said. She had her doubts about it not hurting though. Needles always hurt and she was sort of a baby when it came to them, but she resolved herself to not whimper, or faint, in front of Ty.

He came towards her, carrying a small metal cylinder

device that was clear in the center. He took her arm carefully and placed the device against her skin. She tensed, but only felt a small pulse before a red bead of blood hung suspended in the clear part of the tube. She stared at it, oddly hypnotized, until he turned away and placed the device in a hole that opened in one of the walls.

"How long will the results take?" She asked, sitting up.

"Not long at all. The results should be back tomorrow morning, then I'll be able to map your genome to see if you're a match."

"Okay." she said. Absently, she tried to think about how she would pass the time until then. As if he had sensed her thoughts, Ty turned to her, holding something, and then offered it to her.

"I have something for you." He said as she took it. It looked vaguely like an e-book reader she had owned back on Earth, but it was transparent. She had no idea what she was holding.

Ty explained, "It's called a tablet, and it's a device that holds data. This one is loaded with all kinds of information. I thought, since you're new to space exploration, that you might like to read up on planets, beings, or whatever came to mind. It also has a writing feature which allows you to write your own thoughts."

"Thank you, Ty." She was beaming.

It really was a thoughtful gift. She was excited about digging into the facts of her new reality. She also liked the idea of recording her thoughts. She'd kept a journal back home, and wrote in it when she was feeling perplexed and needed to think things through. Being thrown into space and meeting two hunky aliens felt like the epitome of a journal-worthy topic.

She touched the screen and was surprised that she could read it. "How do you know English?" She asked, puzzled.

He laughed at her amazement before explaining, "Your planet broadcasts everything on waves that travel out into the galaxy. Sooner or later, anyone traveling around is bound to pick them up, so we've been able to learn Earth's dialects, English included."

"Wow!" Lacy said, immensely impressed. "I never thought of aliens being able to hear what's going through our satellites."

"Yeah, it's no trouble hearing broadcasts from Earth. Actually, it's often harder to block them out than to hear them."

Lacy smiled at the implication. Earth sure did love its communications systems: internet, phones, cable, she was sure that aliens must have thought humans a little crazy.

After being shown how to use the device, and being herded out of the Med Center so Ty could work, she found a room with a large lounger to sit on. She started to sift through information and couldn't believe the wealth of content contained in this one tablet.

It covered topics such as: anatomies of all the known races in the universe, scans and data about planets, suns, and nebulas, classifications of spacecrafts, technologies, but the largest section, by far, was on the Arathians. At a glance she saw: anatomy, demographics, arts, politics, language, societal relationships, and there was even a section on fashion.

Given that it seemed like the most relevant topic to her current situation, she started with the Arathians. She read a short summary of the race's history, one that included a lot of violence, but then found that they united their world and worked together to protect weaker planets from races that would take advantage with less noble intentions. It seemed that protection had become instinctive to them. It made sense to her as they'd rescued her, and continued to treat her so well.

Lacy began wondering about the roles of females on their planet. Most of the information had mostly mentioned males. She was shocked to discover that, unlike Earth where the ratio of males to females was roughly one to one, on Arath the ratio was four to one!

Due to the greater population of males, society had evolved differently from that of Earth. Arathians now grouped themselves in familial units, which usually consisted of one female and up to three to four males, but it was common for males to mate with each other, first, before finding a compatible female.

Lacy sat down the reader and tried to wrap her mind around having, not only one husband, but four husbands! In her experience, men were kind of a pain in the ass. What woman would want more than one? Then, she pictured Ty and Kor, and the thought of multiple sexual partners didn't seem so objectionable anymore.

To take her mind off the subject of men, she dove back into the information on her tablet. The anatomy section intrigued her, so she looked to see just how similar they really were to humans. After reading for a few minutes, even with her limited scientific knowledge, she could see how Arathians could be distant cousins. The similarities were astonishing!

Even though they were close to human anatomies, she did see some interesting differences between human and Arathian men. Like the fact that their senses were more acute, they were hairless below the their heads, they didn't have extra and useless organs like appendixes, but the most interesting difference was that the Arathian penis secreted its own lubrication along the entire shaft..

Now that gave her some ideas...

She closed out of the Arathian section quickly and began looking at various other species of aliens. She was amazed at the diversity the universe had to offer. Apparently the creatures that attended her auction were not the strangest in existence... Some were downright freaky!

If humans learned only one percent of the knowledge on the tablet it would blow away what everyone on Earth thought they knew about the universe. She chuckled to think of the people, back home, who didn't even believe that aliens existed.

"If only they could see me now..." she muttered.

"If who could see you?" A male voice said from behind her, shocking a small cry out of her.

Kor walked into her line of sight laughing. "I'm sorry, I didn't mean to scare you. Ty told me that he gave you a tablet, so I thought I would come and see if you had any questions about anything." He sat down on the lounger at her feet and waited.

"Oh, yeah I do." she said, gently shaking the tablet. "This thing raises more questions than it answers."

"Like what? Ask away." He leaned back and rested his arms along the top of the couch, while spreading his legs in the typical male fashion. He looked perfectly at ease, the master of his own universe. Sitting in that position, his chest looked unbelievably broad, and she had to fight her mind from conjuring images of her straddling his hips and running her hands up his chest, feeling all those muscles.

What was with those men and the effect they had on her body? Was it some kind of alien pheromone? She made a mental note to look it up on her new tablet, ASAP.

She looked up his body and met his eyes. They seemed to reflect the same hunger she was fighting inside of herself, so she blurted the first question that popped into her mind. "There are some freaky looking aliens in this thing, but there are some that look quite similar to humans and Arathians. Did you test them for compatibility?"

Kor paused and seemed to be deciding whether or not to let her get away with the obvious change in direction, but he took pity on her and answered, "You're right. There are other bipedal species that are similar to us, but unfortunately their genetic code is not close enough to help us."

"But I'm not you're only chance, right? I mean, you have other options if I'm not a match?" She suddenly didn't like the thought of holding an entire race's existence in the palm of her hand… or in her DNA.

"You're the best chance Arathians have come across in the last twelve years. When we realized what was wrong, we asked our allies for help in looking for a treatment, but so far nothing has worked. We began looking farther and farther away from our homeworld for help. Our ship is one of the farthest stationed, and we will keep expanding our search until we find a solution… Or until we all die out."

At the thought of their race going extinct, and in particular, those two men dying, Lacy felt like something inside of herself get crushed. She suddenly wished, with all her heart, that she could help those men. *Please, please, let my DNA help*, she thought.

Kor must have sensed her sudden change in mood because he got up quickly and offered her his hand. "Would you like to see the rest of the shuttle? I was just about to head to the Command Center, care to join me?" he asked.

She was excited to see more of an alien spaceship, so she took his hand, this time without hesitation, and allowed him to lead her towards the Command Center.

"What is it with you guys and touching?" she asked as they walked the halls. "I swear, I haven't walked anywhere on this ship yet without being carried or having my hand held."

Kor chuckled at her question, but responded, "I don't know how it is in your culture, but we're a very affectionate race. We don't like to be apart from the ones we care about, so we're almost always touching, in some fashion. I hope it doesn't bother you."

She thought about it a moment. "No, it doesn't bother me. I was just making sure you didn't think I was a child that needed to be guided around."

Kor stopped suddenly in the hall and as he turned to look at her, she saw obvious arousal in his eyes. "I most certainly do not view you as childlike in *any* way." He said in a voice that was deeper than usual.

Her breath caught in her throat before he turned away and led her through the door and into the Command Center.

*****

Lacy tried her best to pay attention to Kor as he talked about the different consoles, and what the vid screens showed, but all she could think about was the look in his eyes that she had seen back out in the hall. He had looked at her like he wanted to eat her up.

And she was totally on board with that plan.

She kept looking towards the chair that he had explained was his, picturing him sitting there, all masculine and authoritative, giving out orders.

What is it with picturing Kor seated? She needed to get her mind out of the gutter, now, before she embarrassed herself.

She tried to act as natural as possible as she leaned back against a console and crossed her legs tightly to try and stop the throbbing that seemed to have taken hold in her pussy whenever the men were around. Then she thought of the fact that she wasn't wearing any underwear and that the dress only went to mid-thigh. Images of her bending over a console and showing him her naked flesh flashed in her mind, and she nearly ran out of the room to gain some distance.

Instead she stood there trying to focus on what he was saying. What *was* he saying? Something about navigation? Who cared about navigation, except if it was her, drawing him a map across her body to her breasts and pussy!

Oh crap, she thought. She had to get out of there!

"I'm tired." Lacy said suddenly and too loudly.

Kor stopped midsentence and focused entirely on Lacy. He'd been reciting systems out loud, for several minutes in an attempt to ignore the fact that her nipples had beaded and he could smell her arousal, which had only continued to grow as the minutes passed. Either his little Earther was turned on by the systems of a ship, which he doubted, or she liked something else she saw in the Command Center.

"Maybe you should rest." He suggested. "I'll walk you back to the sleeping quarters."

Kor held out his hand to Lacy and, once she took it, she practically dragged him out to the hall.

She looked left, then right, before sighing and saying, irritably, "What is it with you guys and the color gray? Seriously, couldn't the decorators have picked a more boring color? At least they could have put up a 'You are here' map?"

Kor couldn't understand half of what Lacy was saying, but he could tell that she was frustrated that she couldn't navigate the ship and get to the bedroom herself. He understood her irritability. He had been in a constant state of frustrating arousal, especially from the moment they had gotten to the Command Center.

"The bedroom is this way." he said, gesturing to their right.

She walked quickly down the hall until he stopped her by his door. He opened it by pressing the panel and, instead of staying in the hall, he walked right in.

Lacy stood in the hall for a moment before walking in and planting her hands on her hips. "Hey, where I come from men don't just invite themselves into a woman's bedroom." She said.

She sure is cute when she's piqued, Kor thought. He had expected this sort of misunderstanding and was looking forward to seeing how she would handle the next few minutes. "That's good. I'm glad to know our cultures have some things in common, but actually, this is *my* bedroom." Kor said as he went to the closet, got some clean clothes, and made his way to the cleaning chamber. "But don't worry, we're willing to share." He added with a wink.

The door closing blocked her from seeing any more of the roguish look he was giving her.

*****

Lacy stood there, dumbfounded. Damn that hot alien! It was *his* bedroom? She looked at the bed and pictured him, sprawled out, under the sheets. Did he sleep naked? She rubbed her thighs together in a weak attempt to ease the throbbing, and then remembered that she still held her tablet.

She sat down on the bed and quickly looked up Arathian biology in the hope of finding a defense against their irresistible pheromones. There had to be a reason for her intense arousal, other than their commanding presence... and good looks... and dark wavy hair... and beautifully muscled bodies... that were currently naked in the shower.

Oh God damn it! Now all she could do was picture Kor's bare body, separated from her by a single door. *Focus Lacy*! She forced herself to bring up Arathian anatomy and discovered that her pheromone hypothesis wasn't true. Frustrated, she dropped her tablet onto the bed and laid back, staring at the ceiling as if it held all the answers to the universe.

Why was she fighting her body and this attraction she felt? *That's easy*, she thought. She was fighting it because she had the hots for two men. Two men who were obviously close friends, and colleagues, that were focused on saving their planet from extinction. She liked them both and didn't want to have to choose or cause problems between the two of them. She felt depressed at the thought of never having either of them and was still sulking when Kor came out of the cleansing stall.

Kor took in the sight of Lacy lying on their bed and decided that was the perfect place to keep her. Something was wrong though, she had frustration and sadness written all over her face. What had upset her?

Kor was suddenly determined to erase that look and replace it with something much more suited to her beauty… Like the look of sexual bliss.

Kor moved forward and planned on crawling over the bed to her, but the moment was interrupted when the door swooshed open and Ty walked in, immediately taking in the sight of a tempting-looking Lacy on the blankets, and Kor dressed in nothing but loose fitting pants.

"Am I interrupting something?" Ty's voice was a mixture of laughter and hopefulness.

Lacy sat up abruptly. "No, no! Of course not!"

She sent her fingers through her hair, smoothing it down, in what Kor was sure was a nervous gesture.

"I was just doing some research before going to bed." She seemed to pause for a moment and rethink her words before stuttering out, "I mean, I was going to sleep... on the bed... but Kor says this is his room?" she ended in confusion.

"Yes, this is his room, and my room, and now it is yours as well." Ty said.

"Oh, well I can't kick you out of your bed... wait a sec... you share this bed? Together?"

Kor couldn't help but mirror Ty's smile at the innocence of her question. He had a moment to wonder about her reaction to their relationship. On their planet it was natural, and indeed encouraged, for multiple males to mate with one another. He had friends, back home, who had four males to their one female. *Lucky bastards*, he thought. This was natural on Arath because of the disparity of males to females. Nearly all alien races had accepted their way of life, but there were always the limited few who let their prejudices get in the way. He tried not to think of those close-minded races and hoped that Earthers didn't fall into that category.

Ty seemed to be awaiting his lead on how to best answer Lacy's question. Kor decided that it was always better to be open and honest.

He sat down on the bed, faced Lacy, and choosing his words carefully said, "Yes little Lacy, we share this room, this bed, and our whole lives with one another."

He paused to gauge her reaction but when she continued to sit quietly, he held out his hand to Ty who stepped forward, took it, and allowed himself to be drawn to sit next to Kor. Only once he had his mate close at hand did he continue.

"We've been mated for a long time now, and I consider myself immeasurably lucky to have him." He knew that the love he felt for Ty shone in his eyes. He kissed Ty's hand then turned to Lacy. He feared her reaction because, for some reason, this little Earther's opinion mattered a great deal to him.

She sat very still for several heartbeats before asking, "So... you're gay?" When they both gave her quizzical looks, she rephrased, "You're homosexuals? You only like other men?"

Ty was the one to answer, "No, no, you misunderstand Kor. We are mated, which means we've committed ourselves to each other, but we both still like females as well."

"So, you're bisexual then?" She tried to clarify.

"If you're asking if we're sexually attracted to both males and females, the answer is yes. Nearly our entire population is." Ty answered.

Lacy was having a hard time processing this new piece of information. Not because she had a problem with homosexuality, on the contrary, because she had the problem of getting aroused when thinking about two men together. It was the thoughts of those two men, making love to each other on the bed she currently sat upon, that she couldn't think past.

She saw images of their naked sweating bodies, intertwined, and their mouths clashing, while their aroused cocks rubbed together until spilling out over their hard chests. She mentally shook herself to cast out the images and cursed her overactive imagination for what seemed like the hundredth time that day.

She was finally able to look up, but her heart sank at the sight of them, sitting next to one another, still holding hands, like they couldn't bear to be parted from one other.

They obviously loved each other and, as she thought about the fact that they were in a committed relationship, her chest began to feel tight. She could never get between mates. She wanted them both badly, but now they were even more off-limits to her than they were before. She would never want to be the cause of discord between them. She was stuck.

Well... damn.

"I understand." She said sadly. "Will you please show me to my room then? I would really like to get some rest." *Rest? Ha!* She wanted to be alone as soon as possible to sort out those feelings she had for them both, come to terms with the ache in her chest, and then take the edge off of the clawing hunger before, hopefully, falling into a deep sleep.

The men shared a look then Kor said, "I'm sorry, little Lacy, but this is the only bed on the ship and we're all sharing it."

With that definitive statement made, they moved as one; Kor crawled up the bed and under the blankets while Ty went into the cleansing chamber. Before Lacy knew what was happening, Kor had pulled her up the bed, under the covers, and had her head pillowed on his shoulder despite her protests.

Not a minute passed before Ty emerged, in pants just like Kor's, and crawled into bed behind Lacy and spooned her with his left arm thrown over her middle and his face in her hair. She finally stopped her protests because, as much as she felt like she was intruding on their private lives by sleeping in bed with them, the feeling of them both being wrapped around her was just too good. Maybe she could enjoy their comfort for just one night.

She tentatively put her left hand on Kor's chest and couldn't help but run her fingers, briefly, over his pectoral muscle. That got her thinking about the differences in Arathian male anatomy, in particular, what she had briefly read about their penises.

She tried to make her mind go blank before her

imagination got too involved and she was awake for the rest of the night, laying there, horny, and unable to do anything about it.

Within minutes, their warm bodies and steady breathing lulled her to sleep faster than anything else ever had. Her last thoughts were of how safe she felt, and how she wished she could stay there, with those men, forever.

*****

Ty awoke to the familiar warmth of a body lying next to his. His eyes shot open when he realized that what was not familiar were the lush curves pressed up against his bare torso and the long hair that spilled all around. He looked down and saw Lacy, still sleeping with her head pillowed on his chest, and an arm and a leg slung over him.

He looked towards Kor and saw his mate just beginning to open his eyes on Lacy's other side. He was pressed as close as he could get against her back, with his head on Ty's pillow. When he met Ty's eyes he smiled and shifted to give him a soft kiss.

Lacy muttered something in her sleep and both men smiled at her. Kor reached out his free hand and ran it through her hair. Ty caught the tender expression on his mate's face and knew they were both sunk. In a very short amount of time, the little Earther had become very dear to them both.

Lacy slowly began to wake and stretched her body in a sensual wave of motion. Her thigh rubbed right across Ty's groin and he couldn't contain the small groan that escaped his lips.

She stilled and then seemed to realize where she was. Or rather, *on whom* she was. She turned her head to look at his face and he thought he saw arousal in her eyes.

"Good morning." His voice came out deeper than usual from having just woken up. "Did you sleep well?"

"Yes, thank you." she replied softly.

Lacy really didn't want to move off of Ty. She knew she should apologize for basically blanketing his entire upper body, but when she had felt the hard shaft under her thigh she couldn't seem to make herself move away.

Even if she could, she didn't have far to go by the feel of the very hard Arathian body pressed against her back, butt, and thighs. Speaking of butts... she gave hers a little movement... yep! There was another hard cock pressed against the seam of her ass.

She groaned and let her head drop back onto Ty's muscled chest. *Seriously?* There she was, trying to be a good person, and not climb up those men and beg them to take her, thus tempting them to break their commitment to each other, while they're looking like gorgeous Greek Gods. Gods that were as hard as rock.

Oh... she was in so much trouble! She needed to distance herself, and the only way she could escape the cocoon of bodies was to go over Ty, which would mean she'd have to straddle him, though only for a moment.

She planned her escape then quickly hoisted herself up onto her left knee, shifted her right leg across his hips, and shifted her body quickly over his. What she hadn't been counting on was Kor's arm, that had been resting over her abdomen, pushing down on her back, right as she was fully on top of Ty and pressing her flat against his chest.

Before she could utter a protest, Kor's bare chest was against her back pinning her down and she was unable to escape.

It all happened so quickly that she had no time to recover or get away from them. Kor's lips were right against her left ear. "Going somewhere, little Lacy?" He asked.

Ty must have felt the little shiver that moved through her as Kor's warm breath tickled her ear because he let out a small noise. No wonder, since this position put his cock right against her cleft. If the dress had been any shorter there'd only be thin pants separating them.

"I... I was trying to get up." She lamely stammered.

Kor began placing slow soft kisses against the left side of her neck and jaw. She couldn't help but close her eyes and, for a moment, she tilted her head to give him better access. Then, her eyes flew open and she looked down at Ty, whose own hunger shone brightly in his eyes.

"I can't do this." She whispered.

Ty must have seen panic in her eyes because he took her face between his hands and tenderly asked her, "What can't you do, little one? Be with us? Because your body is saying otherwise."

She shook her head, still trapped in his hold. "No, I can't be with you, either of you."

"Why would you think that?" He asked.

Lacy couldn't believe this was happening. She was pinned between walls of muscle, muscle that obviously wanted her, and she had to overrule her body's desires and stick to her convictions. She was close to losing the battle, but managed to say, "Because I refuse to be a home-wrecker!" At Ty's look of confusion she felt deflated and wilted against his chest. "Yes, I want you both, but I refuse to come between you two. I don't want to cause discord in your relationship."

"Why would you ever think such a thing would happen?" Kor asked from his position at her back. "We both care about you and have wanted you since the moment we saw you."

Ty moved his hands away from her face and rubbed up and down her sides in a soothing gesture.

"It is kind of you to protect us, but sharing you will not harm our relationship. If anything, it will bring us closer together since you're the first female we've ever both wanted." Kor elaborated.

She looked into Ty's eyes and he nodded and smiled. "Give into us, little Lacy, give into your body."

He put his hands on her face again and brought her down until her lips touched his.

Ty felt her reluctance for only a moment before she gave in and kissed him back in earnest. She gasped and he used the opportunity to seek out her tongue with his own. Her flavor was addicting and he vowed to taste every inch of her body by the end of the day.

As the kiss became more demanding, he felt her body start to move in a rocking motion, causing the very center of her to press against his hard cock. He could feel her heat through the thin layers of fabric that separated them and wanted their clothing to just disappear.

One of Ty's hands braced the back of her neck, pulling her against him to deepen the kiss. Her hands, tangled in his long hair, held tight against his assault.

At her back, Kor was kissing her neck, shoulders, and anywhere else he could reach. He ran a hand up and down her spine, learning her curves and loving how they filled his hands. He moved down her body to her legs, stroking them softly before running his hand up to her ass and up her back, under the dress.

Lacy pushed herself up, slightly, off of Ty's chest so that he could put his hands on her stomach. They moved farther up to cup her breasts. She moaned into Ty's mouth as he used his fingers to explore her nipples that had tightened into hard buds. The more he stroked and touched, the harder she rubbed against Ty's body, obviously needing relief.

Kor moved a bit as Ty released her mouth and pushed her up into a sitting position. She didn't need any encouragement to raise her hands so Kor could peel the dress over her head.

"Pink... they're pink." Ty said in awe as he reached his hands up again and cupped her bare breasts. He massaged them, experimenting with their weight and sensitivity before pinching the pink nipples. It made her let out a little cry and arch back into Kor's embrace. He took advantage and guided her mouth to the side for a kiss of his own.

"Are you wet little one?" Kor asked as he pulled back from her lips.

"Yes." She answered huskily, still moving her hips instinctively against Ty.

"Are you aching?"

"Yes."

"Are you ready for me?"

"Oh God, yes, please!"

Kor gave her one last hard kiss then, with a gentle pressure, eased her torso back down to lay on Ty, who pushed her up his body slightly so that he could take one of her creamy breasts in his mouth.

Lacy was experiencing sensory overload. She had Ty suckling her breasts, and doing something *amazing* with his teeth on her nipples, while Kor was rubbing the globes of her ass, his hands getting closer to her core with every pass.

Finally, he dipped his fingers into her pussy and she

was sure they must have come away covered in her juices. She'd never been so aroused in her life and she was afraid that she'd climax with the first touch of her clit.

She lifted her ass into the air, to give him more room to maneuver, and heard his slight intake of air.

"She's pink here too." he said in awe.

Ty paused in his wonderful torture of her breasts to look at Kor. Something heated passed between them before they both dove back against her body with relish.

She cried out as Kor pushed a finger into her pussy and started pumping. Ty pulled her down flat against him again and attacked her mouth, like a man starved.

"I have to have you now." She heard Kor rumble from behind her, a moment before she felt his hard cock riding against her cleft.

"Yes!" She cried out as he slipped through her juices.

"Do you want me little Lacy?" Kor hissed.

Lacy could hardly think through her arousal, but managed, "Kor, give me your cock now because I can't wait another minute!"

She only had a moment to worry about his size, and the fact that she hadn't had sex in a long time, but then he was slowly pushing into her channel and all coherent thought vanished. She moaned her bliss and pushed back against him, encouraging him to give her more of that wonderful cock.

When Kor was fully sheathed inside her, he had to pause for a moment to collect himself because he felt like he was about to shoot inside Lacy with the first stoke. She felt unlike anything he'd ever experienced. She was hot, wet, and fit his manhood perfectly.

Kor looked down and saw Ty, laying under her, watching them and running his hands over whatever parts of them both that he could reach. He had a look of intense arousal mixed with possessiveness that Kor couldn't help but mirror.

"Do it. I want to watch you take her." Ty whispered to him.

That was all the encouraging Kor needed.

He slowly pulled out of Lacy then slammed back in. She moaned his name then pushed back to meet his next thrust. Within moments Kor was mindless from his need. He pounded into Lacy with such force that he was sure he was hurting her, but she kept moaning and pushing back to meet his thrusts while she latched onto Ty's mouth.

Kor was so close and with every single stroke he was rushing towards the ledge, but he was determined to pleasure Lacy before giving in to his own. When her snug pussy began to contract around his cock, and she began crying out her release, he knew he couldn't last a moment longer. He felt the pressure in his balls reach a crescendo and couldn't stop his seed from pumping into her heat.

Lacy dropped completely onto Ty who wrapped her up in his arms.

Kor slowly pulled out of Lacy, unsure whether or not he had hurt his delicate little Earther. She let out a groan as he withdrew.

"Are you ok? Did I hurt you?"

"Hmm... no. Not at all..." She said in a gravely voice, husky from all the moans and cries.

He took a deep breath of relief and stoked his hand over her bare back, butt, and legs. Now he had another matter of business.

He met Ty's eyes and motioned, showing his mate his intentions. Ty's eyes lit up with excitement and he nodded. Together they both clasped Lacy's bare body and turned her over so her back was now on Ty's chest, her legs parted over his hips.

She cried in protest at being moved, and started to get up, but Ty wrapped his arms around her middle to hold her in place.

"What do you think you're doing?" Lacy demanded.

"I want to see if you taste as good as you smell." Kor said as he lowered his head towards her pussy.

It clenched at his words and she suddenly felt very exposed, then she felt nothing but pleasure as he ran the flat of his tongue up along her entire cleft. She jolted sharply when he reached her clit, but he just pulled back and savored her flavor.

"Absolutely delicious." He said with lust in his voice. He bent back her to again and this time stuck his tongue right into her pussy. She cried out as he whirled it around for a moment before pulling back again, leaning over her, and bringing his mouth down to meet Ty's in a rough kiss. She watched, hypnotized, as he shared her flavor with his mate.

"Addicting." Ty murmured as Kor withdrew.

"I think Ty has been more than patient, don't you Lacy?" Kor asked her.

When she nodded eagerly, Kor rocked back on the bed, reached under her butt to grab Ty's pants, and pulled them down his body. They didn't make it far before Ty's cock got caught in the waistband and it was pulled back until it gave way. With an audible smack, Ty's rod bounced back and slapped her in the pussy. She let out a small cry of surprise as he groaned, but couldn't stop her hips from rocking against his hard length.

"Now that's a beautiful sight." Kor said with delight before he reached down and took Ty's cock into his hand, rubbing him back and forth against her slit, watching as Ty's juices mixed with her own.

Lacy tried to wiggle, and get him positioned where she wanted him the most, but Kor kept teasing them both. Then, he leaned forward and took Ty's manhood into his mouth.

Ty growled from behind her as she took in the sight through her spread legs, of Kor's head moving up and down over Ty's length. She couldn't tear her eyes away from one of the hottest sights she'd ever seen.

Ty was clearly at his limit.

"By the Gods Kor!" Ty yelled at his mate. "I can't take it anymore!"

"I'm sorry Ty, but the taste of you two together is delicious." Kor admitted. Then he lowered his head and latched his mouth to Lacy's clit, experimenting, flicking, suckling, and moaning around it. Ty had to tighten his hold on their little Earther when she nearly arched off of his chest.

"Kor, please… please… please." She babbled while tossing her head from side to side.

Ty knew they he and Lacy were both well past their limits of endurance and nearly came as Kor began alternating his mouth between his cock and Lacy's pussy. He knew better than to beg, Kor had gone into true alpha mode, and wouldn't stop until he wanted to.

Finally, Kor grabbed Lacy's hips and pulled her down to align her body with Ty. He looked into their faces while he slowly pulled Lacy down Ty's length.

When he was seated, fully inside her warmth Ty knew that he'd never be the same again. He pumped his pelvis up, shoving himself as deep as he could go. In response, Lacy moaned, "Oh yes!"

When she shouted, "More Ty! Please!" he lost himself in his pleasure and began pumping as hard as he was able into her tight sheath. She felt like wet silk around his cock and he had to concentrate on holding back from coming.

When Lacy cried out again he looked down her body and saw Kor's head, back between her splayed legs, licking and suckling on her clit. She reached down and threaded her fingers into his hair, presumably to hold him tightly against her.

When her cries became constant, Ty had a moment of relief knowing that Kor would ensure that she climaxed before him, but then he felt an extra warmth and wetness against the base of his cock and lower, engulfing his balls, causing him to falter in his rhythmic thrusts.

By the Gods... Kor was taking him in his mouth while he was inside of Lacy!

Although Ty couldn't see Kor's face from that angle, his imagination had no problems filling in the blanks. He could feel Kor sucking first one ball into his warm mouth, rolling it around, letting it go with a pop, and switching to give the other one the same attention. Then his tongue was back, licking all around whatever portion of Ty's cock he could reach before it disappeared back into Lacy's pussy.

Ty tried to imagine how he tasted, covered in her cream and that was the thought that sent him over the edge.

Luckily, Kor knew his body well and yelled, "Come now Lacy!", right before latching onto her clit. She answered Kor with a scream while her inner muscles milked Ty's cock, seemingly drawing out every last drop of his seed.

Lacy lay, completely spent, on top of Ty. Kor gave her pussy, and Ty's softening cock, one last kiss each before pulling Ty out of her and sliding her off Ty's chest and into his arms. He lay down with her and Ty immediately moved to blanket her back with his body.

Her mind was a constant hum of pleasure from the most erotic and fulfilling sexual experience of her life. If she'd known it would be this good with two men she might have looked harder for a couple back home!

Her mind immediately corrected itself, it wasn't just *any* two men that could send her to such heights, but *those* two men. They had irrevocably ruined her for anyone else, and if she was being honest with herself, she knew she'd never want anyone as much as she wanted Kor and Ty.

It wasn't just the way they treated her, but the bond they shared with each other that made the sex they had just shared so special.

She wanted to lay there, for hours cocooned in their embrace, but the moment was interrupted by some kind of alarm sounding suddenly throughout the ship.

CHAPTER 5

Kor immediately jumped out of bed, careful not to jostle her too much, and ran to the closet and began pulling on a flightsuit.

"What's going on?" She asked, suddenly very alert.

"I'm not sure little one, but get dressed please. Ty, hurry and meet me in the Command Center." Kor ordered before he hurried out of the room.

Ty got up as well and tossed her dress onto the bed with a wink. "Try not to worry. Kor was made for this type of thing. He thrives on adventure." He said it with a smile, but she knew that he was just trying to reassure her.

She quickly pulled her dress over the head, grabbed Ty's outstretched hand and, together, they hurried to the Command Center to join Kor.

They found him at his console, inputting commands with a speed that baffled Lacy's human mind. Gone was the intimate lover from a few minutes ago. Now he was all business, and it turned her on to see him in this role of authority.

"Ty, get Lacy strapped into a seat then take over

navigation. Our long range sensors picked up a Voro-Anim ship, and I'd like to avoid it."

Ty went slightly pale as he ushered her over to a seat, slightly behind Kor's, one that had its own vid-monitors and console. He secured her straps and then punched a few commands into her console. It came to life and started displaying all kinds of information in English. He stroked his hand through her hair in reassurance, before hurrying over to his station to the left of Kor.

Lacy scanned everything in front of her, but cursed herself for leaving her tablet in the bedroom. She wanted to look up the Voro-Anim and see what kinds of creatures would cause a male like Kor want to evade, rather than engage.

She explored her controls for a moment and found them easy enough to navigate. It only took her a moment to find the information she was looking for.

According to the computer, the Voro-Anim, whose name literally meant "Devour of Souls" were a horrid race. They were aggressive nomads that searched the galaxy for prey. They attacked without mercy, took all they conquered, and ate the remains of the fallen.

There was more for her to read but she had already gotten nauseous after reading the part about 'cannibalism' and didn't think she needed to read on. She understood that those aliens were basically her worst nightmare.

Thankfully, Ty interrupted her thoughts by saying, "The ship looks like a scout." He quickly worked at his console.

"From what I can tell, you're right, but I want to avoid contact so they don't give our location away. I've set a course away from them, but we need to find a place to hide while they pass."

Alien Savior

Kor hated the thought of hiding like a coward, it went against everything in his nature, but he couldn't think of that now. They were on a shuttle that had very few offensive weapons. Not enough to do great damage to the Voro-Anim's ship, which was twice their size, and definitely had more firepower.

Even with those odds he'd rather stand and fight, but they had precious cargo aboard. He knew, without looking, that Lacy was sitting behind him, over his right shoulder, probably scared, but staying silent to allow them to concentrate.

He had to admit that she was already quite dear to him, and the thought of her in the hands of the Voro-Anim caused him to see red for a moment. He forced himself to remain calm. He'd do anything to ensure that they never got near her.

Kor glanced over at Ty and felt a familiar wave of comfort that his mate always caused. Ty trusted him, implicitly, to get them out of this dangerous situation and he'd be damned if he was going to let his mate down. Ty and Lacy were his most precious treasures, and losing them to the Voro-Anim was not an option.

"I think they've spotted us." Ty said from his left. "They've altered course and are coming this way, fast."

"Damn it." Kor muttered under his breath. He was hoping they'd be able to hide until the Voro-Anim passed and then resume course for the Adastra, but it looked like that was wishful thinking.

Kor stopped trying to hide and brought the shuttle's engines to maximum. Immediately, he began looking for options. He needed to come up with a plan, quickly, before they got into weapons range and the Voro-Anim did any serious damage to the shuttle.

He quickly formulated a plan, but didn't know for certain if the shuttle's shields would hold until they got close enough for his plan to work, but seeing no other options he muttered, "It will have to do…" and sped the shuttle off in the direction of the system's only sun.

Ty gave him a look of concern, but strapped himself into his seat and didn't say anything.

The Voro-Anim apparently had no intentions of ending the hunt quickly because when they got close enough to open fire on the shuttle they didn't aim for pertinent systems, but instead hit random areas of the shuttle's aft compartment.

"Feels like they've got a trainee at the weapon systems." Ty commented while the attacks continued to have little effect.

Kor assumed that Ty was right. "They probably see us as easy prey and are using it as an opportunity to let their less-experienced young practice."

Kor continued on the trajectory towards the sun, only weaving slightly to let the Voro-Anim think he was still trying to evade them. They were getting so close to the sun that the interior of the shuttle was starting to heat up The environmental controls were not able to keep up with regulating the intense temperature.

"Are you alright Lacy?" Ty asked.

"Oh, I'm just dandy. But could one of you please turn on the AC for me? Or pass the sunblock, I'm starting to burn over here." She replied sarcastically.

Kor glanced over his shoulder at her to make sure she wasn't actually burning, but other than a flushed face she seemed to be alright.

"Tell you what," Ty said, "when this is over I'll get you the biggest glass of cold water I can find. How's that sound?"

Kor blocked out their banter to focus on his plan. The sun's gravitational pull was already making it difficult to maneuver the shuttle so his timing had to be precise.

The ship shuddered with a direct hit and Kor

guessed that the seasoned warriors had taken over the weapon's controls. They were probably starting to get concerned about their ship's proximity to the large flaming ball of gas.

The shuttle lurched with another direct impact and Kor diverted more energy to the shields to protect his engines that were in the rear of the vessel.

When the pull of the sun became too dangerous, and the Voro-Anim had not given up the attack, he fired the Electromagnetic Pulse Beacon, which he thankfully outfitted all his ship's shuttles with. The pulse hit the ship directly, and on the vid-monitor, he saw the ship's exterior lights shut down.

He turned the shuttle abruptly away from the sun, while the Voro-Anim's ship continued on its collision course, straight towards the sun. Without any power, they would be unable to change course or momentum, and they would continue to plunge towards the sun until they were destroyed.

Kor turned off the main vid-monitor when it was clear that the Voro-Anim had no hope of averting their fate. He didn't think that Lacy needed to witness more than she already had.

Lacy stared transfixed at the blank vid-monitor that, moments ago, had showed the Voro-Anim ship heading straight for the massive yellow sun. She knew that Kor had somehow disabled their ship and that they had no hope of surviving. She felt a moment's remorse for the creatures that would be burned to death by the sun, but then she remembered what she had read about them. She remembered what they would have done to her, Ty, and Kor, if they'd had the chance.

Ty knelt at her side and, when she looked at him, she saw his expression of concern. "Are you alright, little

Lacy?" He asked. His fingers stroked her sweat-soaked hair.

She took a deep breath. "I'm okay." She said nodding confidently. Now that they were headed away from the sun, the temperature inside the shuttle was almost back to normal and she could breathe without the suffocating heat.

She looked over Ty's shoulder, towards Kor, who was still seated in his chair, inputting commands. He had been brilliant during the chase. She had to admit that she had been turned on while watching him. There was something about him, going all alpha-male and saving her life, that heated her insides.

Ty unbuckled her from her chair and pulled her into his arms with great care. She took comfort in his embrace and hugged him back fiercely. She had come close to losing him, and she wasn't ashamed to let her feelings show.

Ty stood there for a long moment, just enjoying the feeling of having Lacy, once again, in his arms. He had been completely focused during the chase, but now his mind kept conjuring images of Lacy in Voro-Anim's hands. He and Kor would have been killed and eaten, but a female like Lacy... There would have been a much worse fate in store for her.

He held her tightly as he realized how close he had come to losing her. She let out a small squeak and he immediately relaxed his hold, pulling back and giving her a sheepish look.

Somehow, in the very short time that she had been with them, she had worked her way into his heart and become vital to his life. He had expected to feel apprehensive at the notion of falling in love with the Earther, but she wasn't just *any* Earther. She was *his*

Earther.

His thoughts were interrupted by a beeping coming from a small transmitter on his belt. He pulled it off and was surprised to see that the Med Unit was communicating that it had finished running the analysis on Lacy's blood.

"What is it?" She asked, trying to read the transmitter, upside down.

"The results are in." He said. There was trepidation in his voice.

He and Kor had been searching the galaxy for nine years in the hopes of finding a race that save their people from extinction. Lacy's DNA was the best lead that they'd ever had. He thought he'd be happy at that prospect, but his mind was overwhelmed with concerns about the future.

If she was compatible, would he and Kor be allowed to stay with her when they arrived on Arath? Would his people treat her with the respect she deserved? Would they take care of her?

He had an overwhelming urge to hide her, in a safe place, so no one could get close enough to cause her harm or heartache, but he knew such thoughts were pointless. He had to put the needs of his race before his own, even if that meant transporting her to Arath and leaving her there. That's what he'd do.

Lacy was trying to think of why Ty could have such a forlorn look on his face. A moment ago he was holding her, and all seemed fine, but now he looked dejected. Was it the results? Was she not a match? *Oh god!* What would happen to her if she wasn't a match?

She hadn't thought about it before, but the men would have no reason to keep her around if she was no good to their race. What would she do then?

She felt the panic growing in her chest and she had to beat it back down. She refused to let Ty and Kor know how much the idea of leaving them pained her. She just had to hope that, if the time came for them to leave, they'd at least find a decent planet for her to live on. She succeeded in forcing back the tears that wanted to well in her eyes and took a step back from Ty who, of course, noticed the change.

Kor saved her from having to say anything. "Well, aren't you going to go check on the results?"

"Yeah... I'm going." Ty finally said.

Kor stared, perplexed, at Ty's back as he walked out of the Command Center. He had looked upset about something and, at that moment, Kor wished that he had Ty's intuition. He looked at Lacy to ask her, but saw her sitting in the chair and staring at her console with the same sober expression.

What have I missed?

Since the battle ended, he had been focused on checking the shuttle for damage and setting in a new course to avoid any further problems. He didn't want Lacy or Ty anywhere near trouble again and wanted them safely aboard the Adastra, as soon as possible.

Clearly, he had missed something important.

Checking to make sure that all the controls were in place, one last time, he unlatched his restraint and walked over to Lacy, kneeling in front of her. She looked forlorn, sitting staring at nothing.

"We're going to be ok?" She asked in a small voice.

Kor looked at her for a moment longer before replying, "Yes, everything is going to be fine. We're on our way to rendezvous with the Adastra. We should meet them by tonight."

That seemed to get her attention, and she sat up

straighter. "So soon? I thought we would get there tomorrow?"

"That was the plan, but with Voro-Anim scouting in this part of space, I want to get us out of here as soon as possible. I've already sent instructions to the Adastra to head in our direction and meet us."

"What will happen then?" She asked.

Kor took a moment to think about his answer. "Then I will protect you, like I have since the moment we walked away from that slaver. Meeting up with my ship and crew will not change that. It will not change how I feel about you."

CHAPTER 6

Lacy kept repeating Kor's words in her head. *It will not change how I feel about you.* What had he meant by that? Was he saying that he had romantic feelings for her, or that he felt like she was his responsibility?

She couldn't help but hope that he had attachments to her that went beyond his sense of duty to his people. She had to admit to herself that it scared the hell out of her, but those two men were becoming the most important people in her life.

Not just because they had saved her and that she was completely dependent on them. They made her feel protected and cherished, they made her laugh, and also happened to give her the best sexual experience of her life. She felt like she was falling hard for the two Arathians.

She looked over at Kor as they made their way to the shuttle's kitchen. They had decided that they could all use a good breakfast. Amazing sex and evading death, apparently, worked up an appetite, and Lacy's stomach agreed. It let out another rumble as they entered the kitchen and Kor headed to a control panel.

He hit a series of buttons and started listing off the food that was available. Lacy had no idea what any of it was so Kor made the selections. A drawer slid out of the wall and inside were all of the ingredients he needed. She watched his hands, which were a blur of movement as he began cutting, mixing, and heating various dishes.

She was mesmerized by his fingers and hands that had felt so good on her body, but had also displayed the same speed and competency at the ship's controls.

Her core began to throb as she remembered how wonderful Kor and Ty's hands had felt, as they had run them over her skin, preparing and tormenting her, before pumping in and out of her tight body. She tried to shift her legs slightly to ease the ache she felt in her body, but out of the corner of her eye she saw Kor's head whip up and around to face her. The breath left her lungs at the arousal she saw in his eyes. Had he detected her arousal?

He set the food and tools down before moving towards her. She backed up a couple of paces, not wanting to evade him but she was overwhelmed by his behavior. She'd never been the recipient of such a naked lust.

The choice of standing her ground or fleeing was taken from her by the arrival of Ty. He looked from one to another, taking in the scene, and Lacy could tell he was trying to decide whether or not to interrupt.

Apparently his excitement would not be overshadowed because he exclaimed, "She's a match. Her DNA matches ours."

The three of them stood in place for a few moments before Ty strode across the floor, took Lacy into his arms, as his mouth took hers in a passionate kiss.

Lacy let herself melt into the embrace and the rush of Ty's kiss. Her blood immediately heated and she kissed him back eagerly. She felt Kor press against her back and she reached one arm around to hold his head while he lowered his lips to her neck.

Ty pulled back and looked at her reverently. "You're a miracle Lacy. Our little miracle."

Then Ty turned her in his arms to face Kor, and once again her mouth was taken in a kiss. Kor was unexpectedly gentle as he nipped at her lips and slowly rolled her tongue with his own. Then he kissed his way along her jaw to her throat, burying his face against it while he stood there, holding her and Ty.

Lacy felt cherished and she allowed herself to absorb the feelings, holding them near to her heart.

After what felt like forever, Kor pulled back to smile into Ty's eyes. He threaded his hands into Ty's hair and pulled him in for a kiss. Twelve years after the vaccine and after nine years of searching, Ty and Kor had finally found a race of beings that had been seeded from the same creators as the Arathians. Lacy was the first true hope their people had found.

Kor pulled back slightly and asked, "What do we do now?"

Ty chuckled but stood there shaking his head. "I'm not sure. We're the first ones to ever get a positive match on the DNA test. There's no precedence. I was thinking that we should try to contact the Arathian Center for Genome Research as soon as we get aboard the Adastra to give them the results. I'm sure they'll want us to bring Lacy to Arath, as quickly as possible, but there are a lot of tests I can run myself in my lab on the ship."

"Okay, that sounds like a good plan."

"Um… I have a question." Lacy said, extracting herself from their arms. "Do you mean that I'm going to become some kind of lab rat?" She asked, stepping away and folding her arms over her chest.

The men exchanged confused looks, then Kor asked,

"What's a lab rat?"

"On Earth, rats and mice are used in scientific experiments. They're kept in small cages, are given food and water, but are taken out and experimented on at the whims of the scientists until they've served their purposes and are killed. Then dissected." She explained.

She faintly heard Ty whisper something a half-second before Kor let out a roar and was suddenly in her face. He lifted her off the floor by the waist, and brought his face to within an inch of hers. She thought that he looked much like an unchained animal before he gave her a small shake.

"I will never allow you to come to harm, Lacy. You will *not* be separated from us and taken to a laboratory to be used in experiments." His breath was coming in harsh pants. "I would never allow it and would fight anyone who suggested such a thing! You are *ours*!"

She brought her hands up to his face and stroked the hair back from his brow, unafraid of his sudden outburst.

"I know you wouldn't let anything happen to me, Kor. I'm sorry that I even thought it. I'm just scared of the future." She continued to stroke his hair and, after several frozen moments, his eyes lost most of the crazed look. His breathing became more rhythmic and the tension in his shoulders seemed to ease. "I would protect you with my life, my little Lacy."

She felt the breath leave her lungs in a rush as she processed what he had said. Ty let out his own sound of surprise from her right and she looked at him to see if it was a good thing or a bad thing. He stood, staring at Kor, as if had just bestowed a great gift upon them.

Kor and Ty looked at each other. "Does that mean what I think it does, Kor?" Ty asked.

"Yes. If it's agreeable to you?"

"You don't even have to ask." Ty said with a smile.

Lacy watched the exchange with mixture of fascination and confusion, while, at the same time, trying to not be too hopeful. They were clearly talking about something important, something that had Ty beaming like a kid on Christmas.

Kor looked down at her, still wrapped up in his arms. "Lacy, would you do us the great honor of joining our family and becoming our mate?"

The moment seemed to hang in the air and everything seemed to move in slow motion. She understood that they were asking her to do the Arathian equivalent of getting married but she had read that, unlike on Earth, divorce was unheard of. The Arathians didn't even have a word for it. To the Arathians, mating was for life, and every member of a family worked hard to make sure that the others were always happy and cared for. It was everything she'd ever wanted from her life back on Earth. Now, it was a life that she'd never have, but that didn't mean she couldn't find something even more fulfilling out there in space.

Her mother had always said that she'd know when she was in love by thinking of her life without that person. And how painful that would be. Those men were unlike anyone she had ever met and the thought of not being with them was unimaginable. With that, her mind was made up.

"Nothing would make me happier." She answered.

She only had a split second to enjoy the twin looks of delight before Kor claimed her mouth in a demanding kiss.

The moment was missing something. She reached out to Ty and she pulled away from Kor's mouth long enough to yank Ty to their side. He was laughing as she wrapped her arm around his neck, still in Kor's arms, and closed the distance between their mouths.

Ty's kiss was more gentle than Kor's, but just as

urgent. He pulled back to stare into her eyes and say, "You have my heart, little Lacy." Then he looked to Kor, "You both do."

They moved closer and Ty was the one that pulled Kor to him. The kiss they shared was primal in its intensity.

Lacy watched avidly, enjoying her front-row-view of the passion those men shared. They kissed with their entire being, and it was enough to make her panties wet.

If she had been wearing any.

The men pulled apart, inhaled deeply, and turned their eyes to her, their pupils dilated. She knew they could smell her desire and it was *such* a turn on. She rubbed her stomach against Kor's bulge and he groaned. He lowered her slowly till her feet touched the ground.

She was suddenly hungry for something else besides breakfast as she reached her hand between them and grasped Kor's hard length, covered by his form-fitting flightsuit. She'd have to remedy that hunger soon, but first she reached to Ty and ran her other hand down his length. She suddenly felt alive and powerful to have those two men waiting for her.

She looked around the small cooking area and found a short box to kneel on. She slowly sank to her knees, looking between them so they knew exactly what she intended. Kneeling on the box, their cocks were exactly at the right height for her mouth.

She used both hands to first open Kor's uniform, then Ty's, to free their hard shafts. She took her time, looking at their cocks for the first time. She admired how they were the same shade of light brown as their skin, but hairless, unlike the men of Earth. Also unlike humans, her two males were already slick with their own lubrication which she found immensely fascinating.

She nudged them to stand closer together and they immediately locked in an erotic embrace of mouths and hands. She moaned at the sight, grasping their lengths and began a slow stroke from base to tip. Their lubrication was enough to allow her hand to pass smoothly along their shafts.

One of them groaned into the other's mouth as she got to the tips, which did not have the mushroom-like head that she was used to, but instead was shaped more like a bullet. She gave the heads a couple of shallow strokes before dipping back down to the bases.

She was enraptured with their texture and feel, but her mouth watered for a taste. She leaned forward and, while holding Ty's cock at the base, licked up his length and swirled the tip, enjoying his taste. He was absolutely delicious and she dove back for another taste, this time engulfing his entire shaft as far as she could take him down her throat.

She couldn't take him far enough to wrap her lips around his base because, just like the rest of his magnificent body, his cock was long and lean. She took him as far as she could go before pulling back.

Ty thought that he may have just died of pleasure as he felt Lacy's first tentative swipe of her tongue, then he had to grab onto Kor's shoulders to remain upright as he felt his cock engulfed by the heat of her mouth.

"By the Gods Lacy!" He shouted down to her.

She pulled off him with a loud slurp, never faltering in her hands' motions on either cock. She had the audacity to smile up at him, innocently, and ask, "What?"

She didn't wait for an answer, but dove onto Kor's cock, giving it the same attention that Ty's had received. Kor groaned and laced his right hand through her hair while his left was still gripping Ty's shoulders to anchor himself.

Ty heard her moan around his mate's cock and knew exactly what she tasted. Ty loved to take Kor's length in his mouth and to savor his mate's taste, especially while Kor was still asleep and his cock was flaccid. Neither of them stayed that way for long, but Ty loved the deep moans of pleasure Kor made in his sleep-laced voice.

Ty was jolted out of his thoughts by Lacy once again bobbing her talented mouth along his shaft. He never knew what to expect because she was constantly changing the tempo, suction, and pressure.

He suddenly needed his uniform off and tore at it. Kor caught on and helped him before divesting himself of his own. Ty always loved the feeling of his mate's body and couldn't stop his hands from roaming the expanse of Kor's muscular chest pinching one nipple first before moving on to the other.

Kor reciprocated by latching his mouth onto Ty's neck right below his ear, where Ty was the most sensitive. With Kor and Lacy's talented hands and mouths, Ty was already feeling a climax building in his balls. Determined not to come, he bore down on his self-control and turned the heat up on Kor, running his left hand down his torso and next to Lacy's hand, still working his cock, and rubbing on the space right behind Kor's balls.

Kor made an unintelligible sound and punched his hips forward uncontrollably. Lacy took immediate notice and, as Ty had hoped, she pulled off of his cock and started working her mouth over Kor's. Kor caught on to his plan and pinched one of Ty's nipples, hard, in retaliation. Ty yelped, but chose to accept his punishment and focus instead on their beautiful mate who was still on her knees in front of them.

He reached down and started to pull her up and off of Kor, who had started moaning with each thrust. The prelude to his climax.

Lacy made a sound of disappointment at having to let their cocks go, but Ty swallowed it quickly with his mouth while Kor swept his hands up her body to remove the dress. Ty had to release her, but only for a moment, as it was swept over her head.

Kor walked over to the table and picked up one side, moving it so that it was perpendicular to the large padded lounger behind it. He sat on the lounger and told Ty, in a gravely voice, "Bring her over here."

Ty, used to Kor's dominance during sex, walked her backwards until she was standing in front of Kor with her back facing him. He reached up and grabbed Lacy's hips and brought her down to sit on his lap, facing Ty. He encouraged her to lean back against him and used his hands to hook her knees over his thighs. As he spread his legs, hers opened up even wider gifting Ty with a perfect view of her pink paradise.

"By the Gods, Lacy…" Ty managed to say before trailing off and kneeling between their open thighs.

Kor ran his hands down, over her breasts, over her soft stomach, and down farther, watching his dark hands over her white skin. When he got to her nest of brown curls he used his fingers and spread her open, even wider, to Ty's gaze.

"Taste her Ty." he said gruffly while Lacy moaned at his words. "I know how much you want to."

Lacy's breathing sped up the closer Ty got to her pussy that throbbed with want. Every beat of her heart made her clit throb and she couldn't stop herself from squirming in Kor's hold. Finally, Ty was close enough and licked up along her entire cleft. He rocked back and closed his eyes in bliss, then he latched his mouth onto her pussy and devoured her. Kor let go of the lips of her pussy to hold her steady on his lap against the onslaught of Ty's passion.

He cupped her breasts, pinched her nipples, and Lacy let out a cry and almost arched off of him. She could feel it building, she was so close, and was trying to hold it off, but when Ty suddenly pumped two fingers into her tight channel she couldn't help but fly apart. He sucked on her clit and pumped his fingers while she covered Kor's hands in her own and encouraged him to pinch her roughly while she came.

When the tremors finally subsided, she looked down to see Ty beaming up at her.

"That was the best breakfast I've ever had." He said smiling with her juices on his lips.

She laughed weakly, still recovering from her pleasure, and she felt Kor's hard cock against her lower back. She remembered her fantasies of riding him while he was seated and immediately regained her strength.

She was mindful of his manhood as she sat up and turned so she sat straddling his hips. She leaned forward slowly and rubbed her breasts back and forth against his chest before whispering in his ear, "I've fantasized about you on this seat..."

She stopped to run her tongue around the shell of his ear and felt his breath catch. "And also in your chair in the Command Center..."

She latched onto his earlobe with her teeth while rotating her hips and lining his cock up with her center. "Will you let me have you like this?"

Kor was clearly at the end of his control because he put his hands on her hips and raised her enough for his cock to stand upright then brought her back down, impaling her with his hard length. She cried out at the sudden invasion but needed no encouragement, she lifted herself back up and repeated.

Suddenly, Ty was on her left side, his cock aligned with her mouth. She immediately latched onto him, closed her eyes, and began bobbing her head in time to her bounces on Kor's cock. She felt Kor's hair brush her chest and when she opened her eyes she saw him slouching on the lounger to line up his mouth to Ty's cock as well. While she bobbed her head up and down his length, Kor dipped his mouth down to Ty's balls and drew first one, then both, into his mouth.

Ty moaned loudly and wrapped a hand around each of their heads. When Lacy pulled back for a moment to catch her breath and relax her stretched jaw, Kor was right there, taking Ty's cock in his mouth and continuing where she left off. Lacy massaged Ty's balls and the sensitive area behind them.

Their motions became more frantic the closer they came to the precipice and it was Lacy that went over the edge first. When she cried out, "Oh God! I'm coming!", each of the males' control seemed to snap.

Ty thrust into Kor's mouth a couple of times before throwing back his head and shouting his release to the ceiling. Kor had barely caught all of Ty's seed before he gave a final thrust into Lacy's sheath, that was still clenching around his cock, and, he too, climaxed.

She fell against Kor's chest with her face towards Ty, who had managed to slide his way down and plant his butt on the lounger. Kor wrapped his left arm around her and his right around Ty, drawing him closer to their side.

They stayed like that for a while, allowing them all to calm their racing hearts.

Lacy had thought that having sex with two men at the same time would be too intense and too difficult to coordinate, but with these two men it felt natural. Even better than that; she felt empowered!

She was perfectly content to lay there, sprawled across Kor's chest, and be held by her mates.

"So, how long are Arathian engagements?" She

asked after a time.

Kor looked confused "Engagement? What do you mean?"

"It's the time between when you ask me to be your mate and the time we have the ceremony to finalize it."

The men gave each other a look, but it was Ty that said, "Little Lacy, we have no such engagements in our culture. Our mating is already finalized."

She sat up, shocked at his answer, and looked from one to the other. "When did that happen?"

"When you agreed to become our mate." Ty explained. "You see, in our society we do not have a ceremony. The moment when the offer to mate is accepted is the moment it is final, although usually later there is a celebration of the union with our family and friends."

Kor touched her cheek gently. "Do you regret your decision to mate with us?" He sounded so forlorn that she couldn't respond fast enough.

"No! No, not at all. I'm just surprised." When they both relaxed she continued, "You see on Earth, when two people agree to get married, there is usually a long period of time before the wedding while they plan it out. They're considered engaged until the ceremony where they exchange vows and rings before their loved ones. Only then are they considered married, or mated in your words."

"That sounds like a lot of hassle." Kor grumbled.

"Oh it usually is. And expensive. I like your way of settling things better, although I might miss not getting a wedding ring." She held out her left hand for emphasis, but the moment was interrupted by Kor's stomach rumbling.

Ty laughed as he got up, gloriously naked, and started towards the counter where Kor had left the food. She noticed Kor watching Ty's movements with rapt interest and was fascinated by the relationship. A relationship, she realized, she knew very little about.

"So, how long have you two been together?" She asked as she settled back against Kor's chest.

"Why don't you take that one?" Ty said from his position at the cook top where he was heating some kind of dark food that Kor had already prepared.

Kor smiled at her and said, "We've been mated for eight years. We met aboard the Adastra. Ty was the Chief Geneticist, one of the leading geneticists in the search for a cure," Kor said with pride, "and I was the second-in-command of the ship. He always worked very hard, studying the various races we came across for compatibility, and mostly stayed in his lab working long hours. I actually didn't meet him until a few months into our mission when I was attacked at a colony and had to go to the Med Center for treatment." When her look became one of concern he added, "I wasn't badly hurt, so don't you worry."

He planted a kiss to her forehead to reassure her, but Ty ruined his efforts by laughing from his place at the cooktop. "You and I obviously remember that differently. I clearly remember the wound that that serrated sword left in your side."

Lacy's eyes went wide and she ran her hands and eyes all over his torso looking for the scar. She found it on his left side, just below his pectoral and she bent to give the scar a tender kiss.

"My poor Kor." She said.

"Don't feel too sorry for him Lacy," Ty called out from across the room shaking his head, "he started the fight on that colony, and then, after he dragged himself onto one of my examination tables, he refused any numbing medication before I closed the wound. Any pain he felt was his own doing."

She turned wide eyes to Kor. "Is that true?" She

asked.

"No, not all of it. I didn't start the fight, a Grungle did. He was cheating at the game we were taking bets on and I didn't appreciate that. Not to mention that he was also wanted by the local law enforcement, so really, I was doing the colony a favor." He said, smirking.

She looked at him skeptically, but allowed him to continue his story.

"So, I was in the Med Center, all sewn back together, and I could tell that Ty had been eyeing me while he was treating me, so I…"

"Wait!" Ty shouted, interrupting Kor's story. "*I* was eying *you*? You're the one that couldn't keep your hands to yourself while I was closing that hole in your side, and you're the one that followed me into that supply room to run your hands all over my cock, even though you could barely stand from the blood loss."

Kor set Lacy down gently on the lounger before standing up and walking over to stand next to Ty. Lacy had to strain to hear his words.

"You thought I was plenty strong when I had you pinned against the wall with my hand around your cock, pleasuring you till you came." Kor said in a low rumble.

Ty seemed to go soft, probably remembering their time in the supply closet, while his cock stood ready for more.

"Oh yeah, I remember now." He said, still dazed.

Kor seemed satisfied with his answer and smacked Ty on his ass before sauntering back to where Lacy was sitting. Ty had given a little yelp, but then smiled and continued cooking.

Kor rearranged her back onto his lap and Ty brought over a couple of plates, piled high, with delicious smelling food. They both began to steadily feed her small bites from the plates.

"So were you guys inseparable after the… uh…

supply closet action?" She asked with a smile.

Ty laughed, "Not quite, but I was much more willing to spend my free time out of the Med Center's lab after that."

She turned to Kor, "Was your relationship a problem when you became the captain?"

"No. Ty and I were already mated by then and there are no rules against it."

"How did you become captain? Or do I not want to know?" she asked.

He smiled at her a little sadly. "Our captain was badly injured in a fight with a Voro-Anim battleship. The console he was using overloaded and he was caught by the blast. He survived, but was unable to continue his duties."

Kor seemed saddened by the memory and Lacy felt guilty that she had asked.

"We were able to locate a transport ship that was heading back to Arath and they took him back for recovery and rehabilitation."

"Is he alright now?" Lacy asked, scared of the answer.

Ty answered, "Yes, he was able to get surgeries back on Arath that I couldn't have preformed aboard the ship. Last we heard he was enjoying retirement with his mates."

"Good, I'm glad he's alright." She didn't want her mates to feel sad and they obviously respected and cared for their previous captain.

Once she was full, and the men finished every last bite of food on the plates, they decided to get cleaned up in case they met with the Adastra sooner than planned. Lacy gathered her dress and put it back on, but she noticed that she had begun to smell a little ripe.

Ty saw her wrinkle her nose and softly laughed, "Would you like to clean yourself as well?"

She immediately brightened. "Can I?" she asked.

"Of course you can.." He held his hand out to her, "Come, I'll show you."

Kor broke off at the Command Center. "I will meet you later. I just want to check the sensors again." He kissed Lacy on the cheek and strode through the doors, still wonderfully nude.

Ty and Lacy caught each other watching his butt flex as he walked away and had to share a laugh.

"He is magnificent, isn't he?" Ty asked.

"Oh yeah, you both are." She suddenly had a distressing thought, "Do all the Arathian men have bodies like you two?" If so then she was in serious trouble of visual overload if she was on a ship full of them.

Ty seemed to give the question a lot of thought before answering as they walked to the sleeping chamber. "Kor and I are of average height and size for Arathian males, and most keep themselves physically fit, but you're right if you're thinking that Kor is especially attractive," he said with a cocky grin. "there are very few males who measure up to him in terms of physique or mental acuity."

"Then I'm a very lucky girl because I got a two-fer."

She laughed at his quizzical look. "Never mind." She said between chuckles. "I just meant that I'm doubly-lucky because I have him and you. Both prime specimens of your race."

They stopped at the opened door to their room and she took the chance to run her hands over his chest, enjoying the feel of his hard muscles, encased in soft, caramel-colored, hairless skin. She certainly was a lucky girl, especially when his cock started to harden and was soon reaching for her body. She gave him a naughty smile and then stepped into the bedroom.

Ty stood for a moment, thanking whoever may be

listening for the gift of his little Earther, then chased her into the bathing chamber, where she was laughing and fumbling with the buttons of the control panel.

They eventually got cleaned, but not before getting even dirtier than before.

CHAPTER 7

"There she is," Kor said with pride and motioned to the main vid-screen, "the Adastra."

Lacy sat at her console in the Command Center and looked up at the image on the screen. For a moment, the vid-screen showed nothing but distant twinkling stars, then a huge black shape seemed to emerge from the shadows. She gasped, covering her mouth with her hands, mesmerized by the sight. The ship had materialized out of the darkness like a wraith.

"How did it do that?" She asked, fascinated and awed.

There was no mistaking the pride in Kor's voice as he explained, "Instead of the standard gray or silver usually seen on spacecrafts, Arathians build black ships. This feature allows them to blend in with the void of space, especially when the windows are shielded and the interior lights are masked. The Adastra also has a shell that imitates the stars on the opposite side of the ship so we can blend into space perfectly."

"Camouflage." she murmured under her breath.

"Yes, exactly. We're one of the only races that use

this technique. It's most common on our research vessels, like the Adastra, whose primary role is not to engage in combat, but to stay under the radar."

"Lieutenant Simdon to Captain Kor'ijak." Said a voice over the comm-link, startling her out of her admiration of the ship.

"Captain here. How are things on my ship Lieutenant?" Kor asked.

"Just fine sir, and I'm glad that you and your mate are back safely."

"Not as glad as I am." Kor said, sharing smiles with Ty and Lacy. "Gather all of the senior officers in the Command Center. Once we dock I will have an announcement to make and I want all present."

"Yes sir!" The reply came immediately.

"We will be with you momentarily. Captain out."

He ended the communication and began to manually guide the shuttle closer to the Adastra. As they came around the far side of the massive ship, the docking bay at the rear of the Adastra came into view. She saw men walking around inside and had a moment to wonder how they were accomplishing their work without space suits and helmets.

Ty smiled at her surprise and explained, "There's an environmental barrier. We just passed through it, in fact. It's an invisible shield that allows the docking bay doors to be open for shuttles, while still keeping the bay safe from the dangers of space."

"Yeah, oxygen is a good thing." She said, smiling, more focused on Kor and how he was maneuvering the shuttle to safely touch down inside. The moment the shuttle was docked, men hustled over to the craft and began all manner of tasks. She strained to keep them in her sights, but the vid-screen wasn't meant for spying.

Kor felt intense relief that they had made it safely aboard the Adastra without another run-in with the Voro-Anim. There had been a good chance that the scouting ship they destroyed hadn't been the only one in that sector of space. Apparently they were in the Gods' favor since they had arrived without further incident.

Now he had his mates safely aboard a ship that had fire power and defenses far superior to those of the shuttle. With Lacy aboard he was sure they'd get orders to leave the quadrant immediately, and take her to Arath as fast as their engines would allow. But, for now, he needed to introduce her to the crew and contact his superiors on Arath for orders.

When he finished his post-flight shut down he stood up from his command chair and motioned for Ty and Lacy to join him. He held their hands as they walked to the exit, but when Lacy started to slow as they got closer to the door he realized that she looked a little paler than usual. He stopped and made sure she was looking him in the eye.

"What's wrong?" He asked gently.

Lacy knew that she was being irrational, but couldn't stop the fear of what lay beyond shuttle's door. The shuttle had become a safe haven for her, a place of refuge after she'd been auctioned off. It was also where she had mated with Ty and Kor, so the shuttle was special. She knew that beyond that door there was an entire alien universe, and it freaked the hell out of her.

"Lacy, tell me what's bothering you. Why are you scared?"

She was afraid that it she told them the truth they'd think she wasn't a strong woman. They'd think her weak, and those strong men didn't deserve to be stuck with a weak female as a mate. She could lie, and tell them that everything was fine, plaster a fake smile on her face and march out that door with bravado that she sure as hell wasn't feeling, or she could come clean. Tell them the truth and trust them to not think any less of her.

"I know it's irrational, but I'm afraid to leave the shuttle. There's a huge universe outside that door and I'm not sure I'm ready to face it."

Kor took her face between his hands and held her steady while he gently brought his lips down to meet hers. The kiss was tender and she knew that he was conveying more in touch than any words could ever speak.

He took his time with the kiss and only pulled back once her mind had settled down and she had relaxed in his hands. He looked deep into her eyes. "Lacy, you know that I will protect you at any cost, that includes from my own people if need be. Ty and I will be by your side, every step of the way, and I promise that you won't be alone unless you wish it."

She looked over at Ty and he nodded in agreement. She reached out and took his hand, feeling more confident from the touch.

"Alright, let's go face the universe, together."

"Together." Kor agreed.

"Together." Ty repeated.

With Lacy in the middle and her men on either side, holding her hands, Kor pressed the panel and the shuttle's door opened.

*****

The first thing Lacy saw were the overhead lights, the other shuttles lined up in perfect formation, and the twenty crew members lined up outside the hatch. They stood at attention, in tightly-fitted black outfits with large black boots that came up to their knees. They also wore belts from which various tools hung, along with the tools was something that looked like a sort of weapon. She bet they weren't just for show either. Along with the matching clothes and weapons, they all had similar expressions of surprise and were staring at her, so she gave them a small nervous smile.

Kor wasted no time, "Greetings everyone." He said to the assembled men. The one closest to them stepped forward and bowed to Kor.

"Welcome back captain. The officers are assembled in the Command Center as requested."

"Thank you Lieutenant Simdon." He raised his voice slightly and turned his attention to the rest of the bay. "I would like to introduce you all to Lacywoods. She has agreed to mate with Ty and myself and is to be treated with all due respect and courtesy."

All of the men bowed as one and Lacy smiled at the respectful gesture.

Kor did not wait for a reply, and walked down the shuttle's ramp, still holding her hand. She felt strange to be walking through the shuttle bay in only her bare feet, but the area was kept so clean and tidy that she probably could have eaten off the floor.

She was led into what appeared to be an elevator that the three of them shared with Simdon. Kor pressed a symbol on the control panel and the door shut. She couldn't feel the floor moving, but was willing to bet they were being taken to the Command Center.

She turned towards Simdon when he cleared his throat. He bowed deeply to her and said, "I hope I'm not being presumptuous by introducing myself to you. My name is Lieutenant Simdon and I am Captain Kor'ijak's second-in-command. If there is ever anything I can do for you, please don't hesitate to inquire."

She smiled at Simdon and let go of Ty's hand to hold

it out to shake Simdon's. When he stared at it without knowing what to do she realized her mistake and laughed.

"It's a custom on my planet to shake hands when you're meeting someone for the first time." she explained.

He smiled back at her and gently took her offered hand. She gave his a few pumps while saying, "It is very nice to meet you as well Simdon. Please, call me Lacy." She let his hand drop and hers was immediately taken within the warmth of a familiar palm.

"What an interesting custom." Simdon said. "What planet did you say you were from?"

"Earth." She said brightly a moment before the elevator doors opened. She caught a fleeting look of shock on Simdon's face before Kor was guiding her out of the elevator and into what was clearly was the brain of the ship.

*****

Lacy took a moment to look around the Command Center. It looked like the one on the shuttle but on a much larger scale. There were some fifteen consoles and the crew seated at the consoles were performing various tasks. She saw vid-screens, everywhere, that showed everything from ship schematics to charts, and things she didn't recognize. On the far wall was a bank of windows that showed nothing but the blackness of space and twinkling stars.

There were also other crew members, presumably the officers Kor had requested, standing around the room. All activity stopped as they stepped farther into the room and all heads turned in their direction. Lacy reminded herself to smile at the various expressions of shock, awe, and confusion that surrounded her.

Kor let go of her hand and took another step forward. "Since I have all your attention, I'll get right to the point. Let me introduce you all to Lacy, our new mate."

She gave them a smile and a small wave while Kor paused to let the information sink in before dropping the bombshell.

"Lacy is an Earther that Ty and I rescued while on Vox. She has already been tested for compatibility, and the tests were positive."

Surprised gasps and murmurs of wonder swept the room at Kor's announcement and Ty squeezed Lacy's hand in reassurance.

Kor continued, "I don't have to explain what this could potentially mean for our race. Lacy is the first real hope we've had in over a decade. She is a treasure, not only to Ty and myself, but possibly to our entire civilization. As soon as we are underway I will be contacting the Arathian Council to share this news with them, and Ty will take Lacy to the Medical Center to further ensure her health and well being. She is our new primary mission, so I trust you'll all treat her accordingly."

He turned to face her and Ty again and bent to kiss her forehead. "Why don't you take Lacy to the Lab while I get us out of here and brief everyone on the Voro-Anim attack?"

"Agreed." Ty said. "I can't wait to put this quadrant of space behind us."

"Then let's get out of here." Kor turned back to the room and began issuing orders. Lacy thought that he looked completely natural directing people and was glad that his position suited him so perfectly.

"Are you ready to go, little Lacy?" Ty asked, breaking her out of her thoughts.

"Yes, let's let our mate work." She said with a smile.

*****

A few hours later, Lacy wanted to run screaming from the Medical Center.

She was exhausted from all of the scans Ty had insisted upon, but was trying to be patient. Finally, she had had enough and had to tell him how worn out she was.

She couldn't leave fast enough!

He led her though the halls of the ship, past crew members that looked at her like she was the Holy Grail.

It's going to take some serious time to get used to this, she thought.

When Ty finally stopped in front of a door, she was more than ready to take a break from all the attention and sleep for a bit. When the doors whisked open, however, she found a renewed interest in staying awake a little bit longer.

The men's room was not at all what she had expected. There was a small dining area and cooking space over on the right side of the room, the left side had a large lounger and oversized, comfortable-looking chairs for socializing. Beyond that, through an archway, was the sleeping area, equipped with a bed big enough for all three of them. Her favorite part of the room, however, was beyond the bed.

The entire wall was made of windows that looked out to the vast infinity of space. She slowly moved towards them, as if in a trance. The ship was currently passing by a nebula cloud that seemed to hold all the colors of the rainbow.

"It's beautiful." She said in awe. Ty came up behind her and wrapped his arms around her. They stayed like that, silent and staring out at the stars, for a long time before Lacy started yawning and leaning back on Ty for support. She felt him chuckle before he led her backwards to the bed. He helped guide her under the covers and she lay there, on her side, facing the windows for several minutes before her eyes drifted shut and she fell into a peaceful sleep.

Ty stood back, admiring his little Earther for a few more minutes before sitting at a console he used for work, adjacent to the sitting area. His work area was a mess of tablets that contained various books and other publications by geneticists back on Arath, as well as databases of alien anatomy. He took the memory drive out of his flightsuit's pocket and inserted it into the console, immediately bringing up all the data he had gathered about Lacy's anatomy and genome.

His first priority had been to make sure she was in perfect health, and as far as he and his instruments could tell, she was. She had suffered no ill effects from being in a cryo-freeze for the nine-month voyage from Earth to Vox, and now she had also been given the standard inoculations for space travel, but Ty had always been thorough and was taking no chances with his Lacy's health.

He gave her scans one last look and, only when he was satisfied with the results, he brought up her genome. While aboard the shuttlecraft he had been able to determine that she was a DNA match for his species, but his laboratory aboard the Adastra had the technology that could allow him to possibly find the cure for his race. He got comfortable in his chair, opened the files containing Earther and Arathian DNA sequences, and then got to work.

*****

Lacy awoke to a wonderful sensation and fought her way out of the fog of sleep to realize that there was a head of long and wavy black hair nestled between her thighs, casually licking her pussy. Her body jolted in arousal as he licked all around her clit, but ignored the hard little bud that begged for attention.

Kor lifted his head. "Good morning, little Lacy. Sleep well?" He asked, nonchalantly, while resting his chin on her thigh.

Don't stop, she thought. She replied breathlessly, "Yes, thank you."

"Good." He replied before diving back down and continuing his torture session. He licked her slowly and thoroughly, stopping every so often as if to savor her. It was driving her crazy!

She threaded her fingers through his hair and tried to guide his mouth to go harder but he would have none of that. He grabbed her wrists in his right hand, held them over her stomach, and continued his exploration.

"Kor, please!" She cried, but he didn't falter.

Finally Ty came out of the cleansing chamber with only a pair of loose-fitting pants on and his hair gleaming from a recent shower. His attention immediately went to the bed and took in the sight.

"Starting the fun without me I see." He teased. She could feel Kor's slight breaths as he chuckled against her pussy. She decided that Ty might be more receptive to hearing her pleas.

"Ty please. He's killing me!"

He laughed but unfortunately replied, "I highly doubt that, little one, and our mate is not easily deterred." He stepped forward and knelt right behind Kor. "Let's see if I can persuade him to take mercy on you."

She saw Ty wrap his arms around Kor, but couldn't see what he was doing. Whatever it was worked because

Kor closed his eyes and groaned. She was rewarded with him plunging his tongue into her pussy.

She screamed in ecstasy, after being so long denied, but then Kor was lifting himself off of her, and the bed, to whisk off his pants. Ty grabbed her around her middle and turned her so that she could settle her on her knees. He crushed their mouths together in a demanding kiss while grinding their bodies together, both kneeling on the bed.

He broke apart from her to lie down on his back while urging her to straddle him. "Ride me Lacy." He groaned.

She didn't hesitate in leaning forward, and used her hips to line up their bodies. She had a little trouble but, as always, Kor was ready to help by grabbing Ty's hard cock and lining him up to her pussy. She wasted no time, sheathing him in one motion that was effortless due to their combined wetness.

Lacy groaned at the penetration then wasted no time riding him. She planted her hands on his chest for leverage and rode him as hard as she'd been wanting to. He felt absolutely amazing, but when he rocked his hips upward to meet her downward thrust they both cried out at the sensation.

She felt Kor at her back and didn't hesitate to reach back and pull his head down for a kiss. She could feel him running his fingers around the ring of her pussy and Ty's cock, collecting their juices, and not realizing what he was intending until she felt something nudge her ass.

She faltered in her movements for a moment, but Kor wrapped his other arm around her torso and brought his face besides hers as he whispered, "Have you ever taken a male here, little Lacy?"

She thought about her one experience with anal and cringed. "Yes, but it wasn't pleasant."

"Then the male was worthless. We don't have to do it today, but when we do take your ass, it will be heaven." He punctuated his words by slipping the tip of his finger into her hole and wiggling it around.

Her entire body went through spasms at the touch and Ty groaned as the muscles in her pussy clamped down on his shaft. She continued riding Ty, harder, as Kor pumped his finger into her ass.

When the pressure increased and bordered on pain, she knew he was adding another finger, but he lowered his other arm from her torso and reached under her pelvis, stroking her clit. After a couple of strokes the near-pain was replaced by shards of ecstasy and she was immediately at the edge.

"Oh God! Harder… I'm coming!" She yelled at her men. Each increased their intensity and she came around Ty's cock. She dimly heard Ty give a mighty bellow before, he too, came in waves inside of her.

Lacy collapsed on Ty's chest and he immediately wrapped her up in his arms. She thought of Kor and looked back to see him gather her and Ty's come from where they were still joined, wrap his hand around his shaft, and give it a couple of pumps. It wasn't long before he was throwing his head back and white come hit her on her back and ass. Ty moaned as her inner muscles clamped down on him in arousal at the sight.

After he had spent himself, Kor fell forward on the bed and settled Lacy and Ty, on their sides, snug against each other. It took her a few minutes to gather the strength to move from the cocoon of limbs and warmth, but Lacy knew she had to wash the mess off of her back.

As she untangled herself and got up, she watched the two men reposition themselves so that they were still holding each other. She smiled at the intimacy and love they shared before walking into the bathroom.

She was surprised to see that the cleansing stall was different from that of the shuttle and let out a happy cry when she realized that it used real water. She lamented the fact that there was no tub, a hot soak would have been divine, but enjoyed her shower anyway. Maybe she could talk her men into installing a tub later, one that was big enough for all three of them. Oh yes, that sounded like a great idea.

She dried off, but realized that she needed a few other things first before a tub, things like a hairbrush, toothbrush, and other basic necessities. *Too bad there aren't convenient stores in space.* She thought as she chuckled and wrapped herself in a towel, which was way softer than any she'd ever used on Earth, and went back into the bedroom.

Kor and Ty were still dozing so she took the opportunity to explore the rest of the room.

It was larger than she expected, but everything was still gray: floors, walls, ceiling, although someone had tried to break up the lack of color with blue covers for the bed and blue pillows for the lounger. She wandered over to Ty's console and had to shake her head at the complete chaos. She mentally added 'disorganized' to his list of qualities.

In contrast, the other desk in the room was nearly bare, except for a vid-screen, a tablet and what looked like a holographic image of a smiling woman flanked by two men. If she had to guess, she'd say that they were Kor's parents.

She picked up the tablet and activated the screen. It lit up with information about Earth and humans, and she smiled to think that Kor had been researching her. She wondered if he read anything fascinating or if Earth was like many other planets he had visited in the galaxy.

She moved towards the kitchen to try and find something edible. The night before, she had fallen asleep before eating and was famished, especially after her morning exercise. She snagged something that looked like fruit out of a bowl on the counter and moved to eat it on a bench seat near the windows. There was nothing to see except stars, but it was still an impressive sight.

*****

Kor awoke to the familiar weight of Ty sleeping across his chest. He looked around the room for Lacy and saw her, sitting at the windows, lost in thought. She didn't look sad, just contemplative so he stayed in the bed and thought about his latest conversation with his commander, General Kitsom, on Arath.

After they had docked and Ty had taken Lacy to the Med Unit, he had ordered his men to plot a course home. They were now in procession of precious cargo and they needed to get her to Arath as fast as possible. He knew that Ty would continue working on her DNA sequence along the way. No time would be wasted.

After exchanging pleasantries, Kor filled the general in on their discovery. The general's first concern was how he and Ty had come to possess an Earther since Earth was a protected planet, but after Kor told him how they had found her, and that she was in their possession legally, the general had dismissed the cost of buying her and tried to mask his excitement with professionalism.

The general confirmed that Kor had been given orders to return to Arath, but mentioned that he would order the other science ships to continue the search, in case Earthers were not as compatible as they hoped.

Kor eventually told the general that he and Ty had mated with Lacy, and the news was well-received, not opposed as he had feared. Kor ended the transmission, promising to contact the general with any relevant news on Ty's research. General Kitsom thanked him and said that he'd call again once he briefed the Arathian Council on the situation.

Kor leaned back in his chair. Everything was in order and now he had nothing to do but ensure their safe trip home, and lavish attention on his new little mate.

Life was indeed good.

*****

Lacy spent her days reading through the data on her tablet. She figured that, if she was going to be staying in space for the rest of her life, she needed to learn as much as she could. After a week of pouring over data, the men showed up one evening with her very own console, complete with a large vid-monitor. They said that she needed a proper place to work and Ty added that he didn't want her straining her eyes with the small tablet. So every day, when the men left for their shifts, she sat at her screen and learned.

She learned about Arathian history, their allies, and their enemies. She had hoped to find peaceful races occupying the galaxy, but there were good races and bad races, just like there were good people and bad people back on Earth.

She also read about the Grays. She was fascinated with them because Earth was one of their protected planets, and she was surprised to learn that they had been monitoring Earth for thousands of years, using advanced cloaking technology to keep their ships hidden from humans while they studied the planet in the name of science.

That pissed Lacy off! That meant that they had been using Earth as their own personal science experiment for thousands of years and stayed passive while Earth suffered from untold natural disasters, famine, war, and extinctions.

It didn't say anything about them performing experiments on living subjects, but Lacy wondered if the stories of alien abductions were also true. Could all of those alien sightings actually have happened?

The Grays' main objective seemed to be their scientific research, but they were also active members of the Galactic Council.

She also read about the nastier races in the known galaxy and found that, along with the Voro-Anim, was a species called the Lazools. The Lazools were a long-time enemy of Arath that came from a neighboring star system. They had used up their planet's resources and now traveled the galaxy, invading other planets regardless of whether or not they were populated.

The Lazools and Arathians had a long history of war. Arath defend planets from invasion, and the Lazools would take over planets for their resources. It was a strained relationship with conflicts eventually being taken to the Galactic Council for mediation.

A few days earlier she had looked up "Earth" in the Arathian database, curious to know what Arath thought of her home. She hadn't been surprised to find that there wasn't a lot of information, besides a physical description of the planet and its solar system, a cursory description of its inhabitants, and words of caution about its protected status. She was relieved to find nothing negative about humans, just a short comment about them being a younger species. She liked the fact that Arath didn't seem to view humans as being beneath them, despite the fact that Arathians were much more advanced.

*****

A few weeks after they had returned to the Adastra, Ty was ready to beat his head against his desk in frustration.

Another test had failed. To make matters worse, he didn't have a clue as to why. He was positive that Earther and Arathian DNA were compatible, but every time he tried to combine the two strands they refused to bind together. He had tried everything he knew to coax the two together, but test after test had failed. He didn't know which strand was causing the problem and he didn't have a clue how to correct it.

He was running out of options.

He sat in his office, with his head down on his desk, and waited for an epiphany.

He was not the only scientist failing either. He had transmitted Lacy's DNA sequence and genome to the Arathian Center for Genome Research and they were also working, tirelessly, to find a way to repair Arathian DNA using Lacy's, but unfortunately they were coming up with the same results. It was maddening!

He heard his door whisk open and looked up to see Lacy standing in the doorway with a tray of food in her hands. "You always work through lunch so I thought we could eat here together." She said with a brilliant smile.

He smiled back at her, "That's exactly what I need right now. Thank you little one."

She went in and sat the tray on his desk, mindful of the piles of tablets strewn about. "This isn't the usual place for a picnic, but I thought you deserved it since you've been working so hard."

He appreciated the thought but asked, "What is a picnic?" Lacy began uncovering the dishes. Ty did not recognize much of the food and watched as she poured the juice.

She sat on his lap and smiled. "Usually, a picnic is

when you eat food outside and enjoy nature while having a meal. You go to a park or someplace peaceful, spread a blanket and put the food out. On Earth I loved taking my lunch outside in the summer and eating in the sunshine. It was always so peaceful."

Ty didn't miss the longing in her voice and promised himself that he'd take her on a proper picnic as soon as possible.

"Eating here, in your office, isn't exactly like being out in the sunshine, but I thought that it might be a nice change for the two of us to eat peacefully instead of in the Dining Facility with everyone else." She added.

"It's a lovely idea," He said kissing to top of her head. "I needed a little peace and quiet today."

"Is your research not going well?" She asked.

He looked into her eyes for a moment, not sure if he should tell her, but he saw determination in her gaze and knew she deserved to know everything.

"The truth is that it's not going well. Every test shows that you're a match for our race, but I can't get our DNA to cooperate, no matter what I try. It would help if we knew the exact reason why we can't reproduce, then I could concentrate on one section of DNA, but I have to work with the entire genome at once."

For the first time in his life, Ty felt like a failure. He had the future of the Arathian race in his hands, had finally found DNA that could save his species, and he wasn't smart enough to come up with a cure. He hung his head, dejected, and sat there with his arms wrapped around his little mate.

Lacy had never seen Ty like his. In the last couple of weeks his usually cheerful self had steadily become more and more depressed. She knew it had to be because his research wasn't going well. That's why she had planned the picnic, in the hopes of cheering him up a little, but now she doubted her plan.

Her heart was heavy as she looked at him, and she knew she had to make him change the way he was seeing his research. She took his head in her hands and forced his eyes to meet hers.

"Ty, I know that you think that you're failing but you're not. You said yourself that you're working with the entire genome at once, and you focus on one area at a time, but aren't the tests you're running eliminating possibilities?" She asked.

That perked him up a bit.

"When you run a test on a certain area of the DNA strand and it's negative doesn't that just mean that you're crossing one more piece of the genome off the list of possibilities? So, the more tests you run, whether or not they succeed, you're still narrowing down the entire genome. You're making progress." She gave his head a little shake to emphasize her point. "They may not be positive results yet, but they're still results."

She smiled at him and was pleased when he reciprocated.

"You're right, my little Lacy, I shouldn't let myself get so depressed about the negative results. They're not failures, just negative test results."

"That's right!" She said happily and gave him a big kiss on his cheek. "I'm so lucky to have such a brilliant scientist as my mate." She paused to kiss his neck and whisper, "And one that only has another couple of hours left on his shift… When he's done, he can go to our quarters, and I can show him properly how highly I think of him."

She saw Ty's eyes glaze over for a moment before he shook himself. "We'd better eat then so I can finish my shift quickly!" He said enthusiastically. Lacy laughed as he eagerly dug into the food she had brought.

*****

A couple of weeks later, Lacy stood in her bathing chamber, enjoying her shower and the new soap she had replicated. The scent was something she had never smelt before, but it had a wonderful relaxing fragrance and it reminded her of standing outside on a summer's day.

She was washing herself, deep in thought when she passed the soap over her breasts and had to stop because of the dull throbbing pain she felt. She put the soap in its container and cupped her breasts in her hands. They felt the same, but when she gave them a squeeze, there was a deep ache.

"That's weird." She said to herself. Maybe one of her men had gotten a bit too rough during sex. She checked her body but there didn't seem to be any marks, scratches, bruises, or blood.

No blood.

She suddenly felt light-headed and sat down on the floor of the shower. She hadn't had her period since right before she was taken from Earth. Lacy had assumed that since the Arathians were sterile she didn't need protection during sex.

Had she been wrong?

She did a quick mental calculation. She had been on the Adastra for five weeks, and was on the shuttle for three days prior to that. She had also been having sex with her men consistently. It was possible.

She had to know for sure!

She quickly rinsed off, jumped out of the shower, and threw on some clothes. With her feet bare, and her wet hair flying free, she practically ran to the Medical Center to find Ty. Not thinking about whether or not she caused a scene, she flew into the room once the doors slid open and ran for Ty's office. He wasn't there, but she found him in the laboratory, performing some experiments.

"Ty!" She yelled, running into the room and making him jump.

"What? What is it?" He said, calmly but urgently.

It was only then that she noticed the other scientists standing around watching aptly. She was suddenly acutely aware of her appearance and actions. She grabbed Ty's hand and pulled him to his office. The second the door was closed she turned to him, but the words caught in her throat. What if she was wrong? What if she wasn't pregnant? She didn't want him to be disappointed again.

"What is it little Lacy?" He asked, gently taking both of her hand in his.

"I don't want to get your hopes up, because it could be nothing, but I need you to run a pregnancy test on me."

She stood there watching Ty intently and ready to try catch him if he looked like he was going to hit the floor, but instead he handled her request with the same calm acceptance he used to handle everything.

"Why do you think you need a pregnancy test?" He asked curiously.

"Because my breasts are tender, and I just realized that I haven't had my period... my menstrual cycle since I left Earth. I thought maybe it was because my body had gone through a lot. Being cryogenically frozen for nine months and all, plus the stress of being sold and thrown into space... but now I'm not so sure. I think it might be hormones causing it all." She finally forced herself to stop rambling and waited for him to do what he did best.

"Alright then, I'll get the instruments and bring them

in here. I'd rather do it in the lab, but I want to keep this quiet for right now. I am going to call Kor. He deserves to be here too."

"Ok." She said as he walked out of his office. She slid heavily into his chair. Honestly, she was relieved to sit back and let him take control of the situation for the moment.

The gravity of the situation was not lost on her. If she was pregnant that meant that human and Arathian DNA had been able to combine themselves in her body to form new life.

What Ty had been trying to accomplish in his lab for weeks, the three of had been able to achieve, accidently, in their bedroom. Ty walked back into his office holding a device for taking blood.

"I don't know what a pregnant Earther's blood is supposed to look like, but if you think there are added hormones in your system then I will analyze your blood and see if there have been any significant changes."

"Why don't you just let the Med Unit look at me and see if there's a baby?" She asked.

"Because that device is in the middle of the Medical Center, and I don't want to get everyone's hopes up until we have concrete evidence to believe that it's true." He explained.

More and more she was hoping that she was pregnant. Not only because of what it would mean to the entire Arathian race, but also because she wanted to carry Ty and Kor's baby. As Ty started to approach, the office doors opened again and Kor walked in. He quickly came to her side.

"Is everything alright? You said you were going to run a test on her, why?" He knelt next to where she sat but looked to Ty for answers.

"We haven't told anyone else, but Lacy thinks there's a chance that she might be pregnant." Ty paused while they both watched Kor's reaction. He took the news in his typical stoicism, but she knew that his mind was reeling.

"Lacy said that a pregnant Earther female has different hormones in their system, so I'm going to take a sample of her blood and compare it to her initial one to scan for differences. If there are differences, then we can scan her with the Med Unit."

Kor nodded and then took Lacy's hand in his own. Ty took the other and placed the cylindrical device on her arm. She felt the familiar pressure, but was too busy looking at her men, and trying to gauge their reactions, to pay attention to the device.

Once he had the blood sample, Ty bent and kissed Lacy's head before heading out of his office to run tests. Kor stayed next to her and stared into her eyes, "How are you feeling about all of this?" He asked.

"I'm ok," she said, "a little nervous. I'm trying to not get my hopes up." Lacy added. "I always wanted a family, but had never found the right man. Now I have two 'right men' and I find myself wanting nothing more but to make a family with you two."

Kor smiled lovingly then leaning forward and gave her a deep kiss. He poured all of his love and devotion into that kiss, and she felt it, soul deep.

They waited together, saying nothing else. After a time, Ty came back into the office, looking a little more pale than when he had left. Kor and Lacy both stood up and looked at him expectantly.

"Well?" Kor finally prompted him. Lacy clutched Kor's hand, feeling like she could barely breathe.

Ty swallowed hard before replying. "The diagnostic shows the presence the hGC hormone in her blood, which wasn't present in her first exam. It means that she is pregnant."

Lacy felt her legs go weak but was, thankfully, swept

into Kor's arms before she fell. He held her tightly and buried his face in her neck. As Ty came close and embraced her she began to cry. The tears of happiness flowed like a river and she did nothing to try and stop them.

She was going to be a mommy, Kor and Ty would be daddies, and their baby would be the first Arathian baby born in eleven years.

CHAPTER 8

After Ty had the Med Unit run a scan on her body, and it was confirmed that she was pregnant, news quickly spread throughout the ship. Everyone she saw congratulated her, and the enthusiasm everyone showed was palpable.

Ty immediately fell into the role of doctor, and questioned her on everything she knew about Earther pregnancies. She was sadly ignorant of the subject, but Ty didn't seem to be that concerned. She knew that he'd keep a close eye on her health and, knowing him, would probably want to run diagnostics daily.

Kor handled the news differently and had sped off to the Command Center having quickly said something about 'reevaluating-the-flight-plan-to-steer-clear-of-anything-larger-than-an-asteroid-two-feet-in-diameter'.

She knew that her baby would have one of the

galaxy's most protective fathers, and had to laugh at the thought of it being a girl and of that girl trying to date in her teenage years.

Later, Kor told her that he wanted her present when he called Arath to tell them about the miracle, but, until then, she was ordered back to their room to rest. Deciding not to argue with her mates about their heavy handedness, she headed back to their room, sat at her console, and began researching Arathian pregnancies.

She figured that since she didn't know much about human pregnancies, and had no way to research them, she'd look up the next best thing.

*****

Lacy stood in the Command Center, flanked by Ty and Kor. On the massive vid-screen were several people on Arath. Kor had introduced them as the royal family, and General Kitsom, his Commander.

Lacy had learned that Arath had the equivalent of a parliamentary monarchy, where the royal family still had power, but elected officials made up the rest of the council.

What surprised Lacy was to see Queen Lyn'ola, flanked by her three kings. *Three kings!* Lacy thought she had her hands full with two men but this woman not only had three but an entire planet to run. What a woman!

All the Arathians on the screen shared Kor and Ty's darker complexion, black hair, green eyes, and looked to be at least six feet in height. Queen Lyn'ola was the shortest, but was significantly taller than Lacy's five and a half feet. She was a beautiful woman who wore a deep red, flowing dress, and had her hair, piled on top of her head, in what looked like a series of intricate knots. Lacy immediately liked her because she smiled openly and seemed to be very genuine.

The kings were all different, as far as Lacy could tell. They all stood shoulder to shoulder, but one of them in particular, King Racknar, seemed to command attention. He had the same aura of 'alpha male' that Kor had. He had short hair and a trimmed goatee. King Arisus, the second of the three, stood on the end and was very quiet. He seemed to absorb everything that was being said and his eyes missed nothing. King Orius, the third of the group, had much longer hair pulled back from his face and no facial hair. Something about him reminded her of Ty, she suspected that he was the caregiver of the family.

All five of the Arathians on the screen were in shock at the news that Kor had just delivered.

Finally, King Racknar spoke, "That is unparalleled news for our entire race. Congratulations to all of you!"

The queen was unable to stop the tears of joy from sliding down her smiling cheeks.

"You must go, now, to the Galactic Council, and arrive as soon as possible. It is imperative that we request that Earth become a member-planet." King Racknar instructed.

Lacy remembered what she had read about the Galactic Council. It was, exactly, what its name suggested. The council was an alliance of races from throughout the galaxy. There was a central meeting place, called the Council of Planets, where ambassadors from each race met, discussed, and decided on various issues. It kind of reminded her of a parliament, or senate, back on Earth, except that the scale was completely different. The Galactic Council represented thousands of planets.

Planets that were members of the Galactic Council were included in special trade negotiations, treaties, helped protect each other during conflicts, among other benefits. She had also learned that it was illegal for one member-planet to attack another member-planet, and if it happened the aggressor was removed from the council permanently.

The king's order had, both, surprised and confused Kor. The Adastra was a science ship. There were no political representatives aboard.

"My king, I do not understand why that requires our attendance. Surely Ambassador Rexvan is better qualified than we are to make such a request before council."

The three Kings shared a look for a moment before King Racknar spoke, "We think it best that you work together, with the ambassador, to ensure success. Earth must be under the alliance's protection, as soon as possible."

"Is there something you're not telling us?" Kor asked his leadership. Normally he wouldn't have been so outright with the royal family, and his commanding officer, but these were unusual times.

General Kitsom answered, "We believe that once word gets out, and no doubt it will, that Earthers may be the key to our survival the Lazools will attack Earth to ensure our extinction."

Lacy gasped, and Kor saw Ty put his arm around her in support.

"They have been trying to destroy us for decades, so there was no race happier than the Lazools when we discovered the effects of the vaccine. They've been failing for decades to eradicate our race, and we helped them by almost destroying ourselves." General Kitsom explained. There was barely-hidden loathing in his voice.

King Racknar continued, "They've been waiting patiently for us to die, one at a time, but now we have hope. Earth is the source of that hope and they will do anything in their power to make sure our extinction is absolute."

Lacy felt sick to her stomach with the realization that her home might be in danger from an alien race and that humans had no hope of defending themselves against. Earth was still so busy fighting amongst themselves, that they would have no hope of fighting against aliens.

It would be a slaughter.

Lacy's temper flared, "Those bastards!"

Queen Lyn'ola agreed in that soft voice of hers, "Yes. Our thoughts exactly, my child."

"What can we do to stop them?" Lacy asked, suddenly filled with a powerful determination. There was no way she'd let her planet face extermination alone.

"You must go to the council at once." Replied the queen.

Kor spoke up, "We are honored with this task, but certainly there are other, more suitable ships with political figures aboard that can be of better help to our Ambassador?"

King Arisus spoke for the first time, "We're afraid that is not possible. You must go. One of the requirements to join the Alliance is that a representative of the petitioning planet must be present. Lacy is the only option for us as a representative."

Lacy stood staring at King Arisus. "You mean that I have to go before the Council of Planets and make the request?"

"Yes, you're the only Earther we know of that's off-planet and, therefore, the only one who can." King Arisus replied.

Talk about pressure, she thought. Lacy steeled herself

before saying, "Okay, I'll do it." Then wondered what the hell she'd gotten herself into.

*****

The next few days went by in a blur. The Adastra made great time traveling to meet with the Galactic Council, which was situated on an ocean world with one large island.

When the Alliance was formed thousands of years ago, they had built a large building to house the Council of Planets, and apartments for the Ambassadors to use, on that planet. Over time, a city had formed around the alliance's building. Now, it one of the safest cities in the galaxy.

Kor and Ty spoke daily with the Arathian ambassador, Rexvan, and formulated a strategy for gaining Earth entry into the alliance. Lacy let them work out the details while she tried to learn as much as she could about the Council of Planets where she would speak. In truth, she couldn't wait to see it!

The Alliance was made up of over four hundred races, which occupied thousands of planets throughout the galaxy. To make matters more difficult, each race had their own atmospheric requirements. For instance, Earthers and Arathians both breathed oxygen, but she read about other species whose atmospheres were comprised of nitrogen, helium, carbon dioxide, and more. There were several species represented that lived under water, and there was even one that survived, surrounded by magma.

It was a fascinating system of government and Lacy's excitement grew, day by day.

One morning, when she was getting dressed and fighting off the latest waves of morning sickness, Ty walked into their bedroom. He immediately saw her gaunt appearance and guided her to sit on the bed.

"Is it bad this morning my love?" He asked, concerned.

"It's bad every morning, afternoon, and evening," she tried to say nonchalantly, but it sounded hollow, even to her. Ty had offered her a medicine used on Arath to help pregnant females with nausea, but Lacy was reluctant to take something meant for an Arathian while she was pregnant. She didn't know how it would affect her, and so she had refused, until her symptoms became so debilitating that she couldn't handle them.

"I'll be fine in a moment." She said reassuringly. "It comes and goes in waves, and this one will be over soon, then I'll finish getting dressed and we can go meet Ambassador Rexvan."

Ty kissed the top of her head, but he wasn't fooled. He knew she was miserably sick, but staying strong for everyone's sake. He had been watching her closely to make sure she was getting enough nutrition and had been feeding her food that was high in calories since she was eating so little. The only items she seemed to want to eat were cravings for weird combinations of foods, like ice-cream with pickles. He hoped that she got past this stage of the pregnancy quickly.

Truthfully, he didn't want her anywhere near the Galactic Council or the stress of trying to save Earth, but there was no real choice in the matter. She was the only Earther and, thus, the only one who could make the petition. He would just have to keep a close eye on her and remove her if she seemed to get too uncomfortable.

A moment later she was up and putting on the dress that she had replicated the day before. Lacy had said something about 'looking the part'. Ty didn't know what that meant, but she had said that she wanted to replicate some new clothes and he had been more than happy to indulge.

He had to admit that her efforts had paid off. She looked stunning in the long sleeved, formfitting, black dress she had chosen. She also said something about wanting to match the formfitting flightsuits that Arathians used as uniforms, but he hadn't paid much attention because he was too busy admiring how the fabric seemed to embrace her every curve, and end at mid-thigh. The knee-high black boots she had chosen completed the outfit.

She caught him staring at her and turned slowly in a circle. "How do I look?"

Ty bounded off the bed and gave in to the temptation to run his hands down her body. "You look beautiful my love. Good enough to eat." He punctuated the remark by nibbling on her neck, right below her ear, a place that he knew she loved. Luckily, or unluckily, Kor walked in at that moment; any longer and Ty wouldn't have been able to stop.

"You'll have to wait until later for that." Kor teased. "It's time to meet Ambassador Rexvan."

Lacy all the sudden grew nervous and grabbed Ty's hand for support. Kor was at her side a moment later, taking her face in his hands.

"Will you be able to do this, little Lacy?"

She gave him a smile, "Yes, I'm going to be alright. I'm just a little nervous."

Kor nodded and then lowered his head for a gentle kiss. He pulled back, kissed Ty, and took Lacy's hand.

Then, he lead his mates to the shuttle.

*****

Kor was truly amazed at the view during their decent

to the planet. At first, all that could be seen was the vast blue ocean. Slowly a tiny island, that grew larger and larger the closer they got to it, came into view. At the center of the island-city, sprawled the circular shaped building that housed the Galactic Council.

It was a massive structure that spread out in all directions, with gardens and pools, throughout the grounds. There were many small domes that were topped with symbols, representing each of the races. Some were flags and, some, holographic images. Kor easily spotted Arath's colors and piloted the shuttle in that direction.

After landing the shuttle and opening the hatch, they found Ambassador Rexvan waiting for them.

He was not what Kor had expected.

He was barely older than Kor with tied-back, shoulder-length hair. He had on the typical Arathian dark pants and tall boots, though he wore a loose black shirt. He had an warm smile, but his eyes were the sharp eyes of an Arathian alpha male and Kor had to feel sorry for anyone that opposed him in the game of politics.

"Welcome to the Galactic Council, Captain Kor'ijak." He said in welcome, bowing deeply at the waist.

Kor bowed back in respect. "Thank you for hosting my mates and I, ambassador. Let me introduce Tyrelian and Lacy, of Earth."

Rexvan once again bowed deeply. "It is a pleasure to have you, and an honor to meet your newest mate. She is such a treasure to the entire species." He smiled broadly at Lacy, then gestured towards a large doorway, "Please, let me show you inside where we can speak more openly."

Kor understood the underlying message of the ambassador's words. *Let's go inside so we can talk without others overhearing.*

Kor, Ty, and Lacy followed the ambassador off the landing pad and into the apartments. They were led into a sitting room with an oversized Arathian lounger and some deep-cushioned chairs, set apart with a table in the middle.

Everything, from the furniture, to the art on the walls, came from Arath and was chosen for comfort, not opulence.

"Please, have a seat. Would you like something to drink? Eat?" The ambassador asked.

"No thank you, we ate on the Adastra before coming to the planet." Ty replied.

The ambassador gestured towards the lounger. Kor and Ty sat, flanking Lacy, who was still admiring the surroundings while she sat.

"You have a lovely home, Ambassador Rexvan." She said.

"Thank you, and please call me Rex. I save the ambassador stuff for official business only." He said with a large smile as he sat in one of the chairs facing the lounger. Lacy smiled at the ambassador and Kor knew that she and Rex were going to get along just fine.

"I have to admit that your apartment is not at all what I was expecting." She said.

Rex chuckled before replying, "We're able to decorate the apartments however we choose while we live here, and I chose to treat it as I would my home. Other ambassadors seem to choose lavish furnishings, meant to impress, but I don't think I need that. *I'm* the one that should impress guests or other diplomats, not my rugs or chandeliers."

He stopped to pour himself a glass of dark liquid. "I also see no need to spend money on such things. I prefer that the money be used on Arath for genetic studies, to help find a cure."

"That's a wonderful thing to do." Lacy said.

"There's no point in me amassing a small fortune if I have no children to pass it to when I die. What's our purpose in life if not to provide a better future for the next generation?" Rex seemed to sum up everything in that single sentence.

Ty spoke up, "Speaking of children, that's why we are here, isn't it?"

"Yes, congratulations to you all on Lacy's pregnancy!" Rex said enthusiastically. "Once it's announced publically in front of the Council of Planets this afternoon, you will give hope to every Arathian."

"It will also intensify the conflict between Arath and Lazool." Kor commented.

"Yes, it will do that as well." Rex nodded in agreement. "That is one of the reasons why we must try and get Earth into the alliance, and ensure the planet's protection, as soon as possible."

They talked strategy for a while before an older Arathian male came into the room. "I'm sorry to interrupt, sir, but it's nearly time to begin."

"Thank you, Vorman. Shall we?" Rex asked, standing and motioning for everyone to exit the room.

Lacy's heartbeat sped up as she stood, and followed Rex down the hall and through a massive, gilded door.

When the door slid open she expected a hallway, or patio, on the other side, but instead the doorway led directly into a small, oval-shaped room with glass walls.

She recognized the pod from pictures she'd seen on her tablet when she had been investigating the council. There was a console at the far end of the small room, opposite the door, and several comfortable looking chairs for them to sit in. She was directed inside, and asked to sit as the door closed soundlessly.

"I don't understand... Aren't the pods used in the Council of Planets?" Lacy asked Rex.

"They are, but since many ambassadors require different atmospheres, the pods take representatives from their apartments to anywhere they need to go, including the council chamber." Rex explained as he inputted commands into the console.

Rex sat down, joining the three of them, while the pod began moving on its own. Lacy was instantly impressed by the ease of travel. Back on Earth, companies hadn't even been able to perfect technology for self-driving cars!

"They're like a self-contained bubble." She said in amazement as they sped past other buildings.

All the men smiled at her, as she watched, enthralled, the sights of the alliance's city. Everything looked clean, manicured, and well-maintained. Some gardens had flowers that looked larger than her body! There were paths laid out throughout the gardens and she wished that they had time to stop and enjoy the beauty.

Just over the tops of some large trees, Lacy could see was the domed roof of the central building that she assumed housed the Council of Planets. The pod continued its trip towards the central structure but soon slowed as it came to a massive arch with enormous pillars, flanking it on either side.

As the pod moved inside, it took Lacy's eyes a moment to adjust to the change in light. She saw that the pod was traveling down a large hallway. A moment later it slowed to a stop. She was just about to ask what was going on, but the pod began an abrupt vertical climb. Lacy was deeply happy that the floor of the Pod wasn't clear glass.

She hated heights.

Finally, it slowed in front of an empty space in the wall. The pod slowly moved forward and with a soft clamping sound, it came to rest. Lacy gasped at the sight of the massive Council Chamber and stood to move closer to the front of the pod to get a better view.

The chamber was enormous and was lined with archways containing pods. About half of the docks were occupied, but more pods were arriving with each passing moment. Inside the others she saw aliens of every color and shape and she was particularly fascinated by one to their right. It looked like it was full of water and inside there were aliens that reminded her of jellyfish.

She reminded herself that each individual was an ambassador of a planet and held an equal weight in the Galactic Council, even if they didn't look like it.

Once all of the docks were occupied a final pod emerged from floor at the center of the room. Unlike the others, this pod did not have a clear dome, it was open and only one individual occupied it.

The three men joined her at the front. Rex explained, "That is the Council Leader. He remains totally neutral on topics and leads the proceedings, allowing us to have an orderly discussion."

Lacy had expected to hear the room quiet at his arrival, but she realized that she couldn't hear anything outside of their own pod. "But, how can you have a discussion when you can't hear anything?" She asked.

"Right now we can't hear anything because the pods block all exterior sounds. Only the Council Leader has the controls that activate the sound, and allow ambassadors to address the entire council." Rex explained.

Lacy thought that it was such an interesting concept. It allowed the ambassadors to be heard without interruption. She felt a wave of nervousness sweep over her at the thought of addressing all of those aliens to plead Earth's case. She steeled herself, she knew that it had to be done.

"Greetings ambassadors," the Council Leader began. "I will begin the Council Meeting by turning the floor over to Ambassador Rexvan, of Arath, who has asked to address the council."

Lacy saw the Council Leader hit a series of commands and a symbol was illuminated on their pod's console, meaning that the entire Council of Planets could now hear them. Lacy swallowed a lump in her throat and prayed that her morning sickness didn't choose that exact moment to act up.

"Thank you, Council Leader." Rex began. "I have requested to speak because I have good news and something very important to discuss with you all."

Lacy was impressed with the way he took command and, with just a few words, demanded the attention of all present. In many ways, Rex reminded her of Kor.

"Firstly, you are all aware of the genetic problems our species has been facing. Many of your planets have been aiding us in trying to find a cure, it is something for which we are eternally grateful. Today, I am pleased to report that one of our science ships has had a major break-through."

He held his hand out towards Lacy, "This is Lacy, of Earth. She was stolen from her world by a Blattarian, who auctioned her as a slave on Vox. Two Arathians saved her, and they are now mated. They discovered just a few days ago, that she is pregnant with their child."

Rex paused to let the gravity of the news settle over the room.

Lacy couldn't hear what the ambassadors were saying inside their pods, but she looked around at expressions of shock, happiness, and some races displayed what could only be, hostility. She recognized the blue-skinned Lazools and all she saw was outright hatred.

Rex continued, "As wonderful as this news is for our

race, our scientists have unfortunately not been able to combine Earther and Arathian DNA in our labs. This means that Earthers are invaluable to the survival of our species. For this reason, I am making a formal request for Earth to join the Galactic Council."

Lacy was glad she could not hear what the other races were saying because she could see their responses and many of them were not positive.

The Council Leader was the one to speak next. "You're request has been officially noted, but I'm afraid that Earth does not meet the criteria to join the alliance."

"With all due respect, I do not agree." Rex replied. "The covenant clearly states the following: one, a member of the species must be present to make the request. Two, the petitioning planet must have an individual serve as ambassador, and three, have another ambassador, from a member-planet, second the request. Earth has met all three of these criteria. Lacy is the Earther present who will also serve as ambassador, and Arath seconds the request."

The Council Leader seemed to take a moment to think before turning to a pod to the left of the Arathians' and address the ambassador inside. "As Earth is currently under your protection, what does the Grays ambassador have to say on this issue?"

Lacy was surprised to see that the Grays' ambassador was the exact image of what humans back home imagined. It wore no clothing and stood about four feet tall, with a slender gray-colored body and limbs. Its head was large and it had large, black, almond-shaped eyes.

It had a small mouth, but when it spoke, its voice was melodic. "It is true that they have met certain criteria, such as having a representative and support from a member planet, but this one Earther is not a representation of the entire population of Earth. It says in the alliance's charter, rule number 3.1, subsection 3.156, that an ambassador must be a representation of the entire population of the planet."

The Gray paused for a moment before explaining, "Earthers are not a united species. They are divided into countries, which have their own sets of laws. They do not have a central planetary government, or leader, and even today there are wars between countries, throughout their world."

The Council Leader turned to the Arathian pod again and addressed them, "Is this assessment correct, Lacy of Earth?"

She stood, frozen by the question. If a planet belonging to the Alliance was required to have a central government in order to be included, then Earth definitely did not meet the criteria. The Grays' ambassador was right, there were wars raging, at that very moment, over land, people, oil, power, and greed.

She was racking her brain, trying to find a way around the question, or to evade it completely, but the truth was blinding. No wonder some species considered humans to be barbarians. They couldn't handle politics on their own planet, much less be involved in the politics of the galaxy.

"Yes sir." She answered. "What the ambassador of the Grays has said about Earth is true, but I would ask that the council not punish Arath just because Earth is a younger planet and we have not yet learned how to unite our people. My mates and I are proof that Arathian and Earther DNA can be combined to form new life. Our two planets and races are now irrevocably connected; to allow harm to come to Earth is to allow harm to come to Arath."

Kor stood at Lacy's side and was, once again,

impressed with his mate. She was standing tall, addressing the council with confidence, even though he could feel the slight tremble in her body. She was a pillar of strength and he found himself, again, thanking the Gods for gifting him with such a treasure. He looked over her head to Ty who looked back at him with a warm smile.

The Council Leader interrupted the moment. "You have made a valid point. Arath is a member of this council, and if Earth is the key to their survival, we have to decide if that entitles Earth to special consideration."

"Council Leader, may I make once more comment on the matter or Earth?" Asked the Grays' ambassador.

"Proceed." The leader replied.

"I would like to remind the council that the Grays have first rights to Earth, this cannot be forgotten, or ignored. We claimed it as ours in the name of science, thousands of years ago, and as such, any claims Arath makes on the planet are secondary."

Kor couldn't help but feel enraged that the ambassador believed that scientific observation of Earth, and its inhabitants, was more important than the survival of the entire Arathian species. The Grays were a race driven by logic and scientific discovery, but seemed to care very little about the well-being of other races. They had always seemed like a troublesome species to him.

"We shall reconvene tomorrow to decide on the issue of Earth, for now, let us move on to other issues." The Council Leader continued to talk, but Kor was no longer listening.

"Is that it?" Lacy asked, clearly shocked.

"For today, yes." Rex replied. "It gives us the chance to have meetings with other ambassadors to see if we can come up with a solution on our own, without taking up the time of the entire council. Tomorrow we will vote and know the outcome."

When the Council of Planets finally adjourned for the day, their pod took them back through the complex of buildings to Rex's apartments. He wasted no time going straight to his large vid-screen to contact the Grays' ambassador for a private conference.

Kor saw the dark circles under Lacy's eyes. He walked over and kissed her gently on her forehead. "Ty, why don't you take Lacy and lay down for a while, until dinner."

Ty nodded then took Lacy's shoulders in his hands and guided her to the sleeping chamber they'd be given.

*****

That night Rex spent hours talking with other ambassadors, trying to gain support for Earth. Most were sympathetic to the Arathian plight, but unwilling to bend the rules regarding entrance into the alliance. The following day, when the vote occurred, the council did not rule in their favor.

They adhered to their point that Earth needed to have a unified government first, before being allowed into the alliance. Lacy told them that unification of the Earth's governments was impossible in the near future and, trusting that she knew more of Earther politics than he did, Kor deferred to her wisdom on the issue and contacted Arath with the despairing news.

Rex did his best to cheer everyone up by hosting a dinner, prepared by Vorman, his assistant. He served Arathian dishes and ales, and it wasn't long before the men began telling stories about their childhoods. Even though Rex, Kor, and Ty all grew up in different areas of the planet they all seemed to have a penchant for getting into trouble as children.

Boys will be boys, Lacy thought to herself.

Rex was just finishing a story about how he used to play tricks on his older siblings when Vorman walked into the sitting room, escorting two Arathian guards.

Kor had seen guards posted around the Arathian apartments, but they had always stayed in the shadows, silently keeping everyone safe. Seeing them openly enter the room, put Kor on alert.

Rex immediately stood up from his chair, "What is it?" He asked.

One of the guards took a step forward and bowed before saying, "Ambassador Rexvan, we were in the city doing our usual sweeps and we overheard a small group of Lazools. They were part of the crew onboard a Lazool spacecraft, and were complaining that they were stuck on this planet, serving the Lazool ambassador while one of their battlecruisers was heading for Earth. They were lamenting the fact that they could not take part in the action."

"Did you hear anything else? Where the battlecruiser was coming from? When they were leaving? Anything?" Kor asked.

"No Captain Kor'ijak. They were angry about not taking part in the battlecruiser's mission, but they did not go into detail. I'm sorry that we could not learn more." The guard said.

"No, you did an excellent job in bringing us this information. Please, go back into the city and see if you can learn anything else." Rex instructed.

The guards bowed together and left the room with Vorman following in their wake. Rex and Kor shared looks, but it was Lacy that spoke first.

"They're going there to kill all Earthers so you can't save your race, aren't they?" She asked.

"Yes, I think so." Kor answered as he sat down next to her on the lounger. Kor wanted nothing more to take Lacy and Ty someplace safe. He wanted to spare Lacy the heartache that was sure to come, but he knew that she needed to be treated as an equal in their relationship. Keeping the truth from her would be insulting and would show that he didn't think she was strong.

Instead of lying, he took her hands in his and looked into her eyes as he spoke. "Yesterday, when we announced to the council that you are pregnant, we knew the Lazools would likely see Earth as a threat because it can save Arath. When the council didn't allow Earth to join, they must have decided to attack Earth since it's a much easier target than the Arathian homeworld. Earth can't defend itself against an attack from space."

"But I thought Earth was under the protection of the Grays." She said, confused. "Won't they stand up to the Lazools?"

Rex was the one who answered, "The Grays have, historically, only shown interest in their experiments. Their interest in Earth is purely scientific and I'm not sure they would protect the planet if conflict arose."

He paused for a moment considering something as he paced around the room. "I'm not even sure they *can* protect Earth. They appear to be pacifists by nature and, while they have the best cloaking devices in the galaxy, I've never heard news of them being engaged in any conflict. I don't even think they have weapons."

"Then we have to go to Earth and defend it!" Lacy said confidently. "Without help from space, Earth will be destroyed. I can't sit here and allow that to happen."

She stood up and turned to face Kor and Ty. "I say we get back to the Adastra and head for Earth. We're closer to it than Arath is, so we're the closest ship. Hopefully we can slow the Lazools down long enough for reinforcements to arrive. In the meantime, we can contact the Grays and see if they can help us. If not, at least they'll have fair warning that a battlecruiser is on its way to Earth."

Kor stared at his mate and felt overwhelming pride in her courage and determination. She was right, the Adastra was the closest ship to Earth, by a week, but it was still a nine-month voyage.

Suddenly Kor thought of something; it was nine months by ship from this part of the galaxy, where the Grays' homeworld was, to Earth. How did the Grays travel there so often for their experiments and observations?

The only explanation was that they had to have control over a wormhole that allowed them to get there quickly. If he could negotiate with the Grays to tell him where the opening was on this side of space, then their travel time could be cut down significantly and they could beat the Lazools to the planet and set up some sort of defense.

With his plan formulated, Kor went to the vid-screen to contact the Grays' ambassador, ready to beg if necessary.

CHAPTER 9

A few hours later and Kor, Ty, and Lacy were back aboard the Adastra and heading towards Earth as fast as their engines could take them. Kor had spoken with the Grays' ambassador at length before leaving and he had finally been given the coordinates for the wormhole. The travel time would be cut down, from nine months to just eight days.

The ambassador had been extremely reluctant to give Kor the wormhole's coordinates, but he had argued that without help from the Arathians, Earth would certainly be destroyed, along with the Grays' scientific studies. Kor had prevailed with logic, and felt better in that he seemed to be getting the hang of talking to the strange little aliens.

The bad part of using the wormhole was that it was slightly unstable, which made for a bumpy ride. As the Adastra made its way to the wormhole's coordinates, the Grays offered to send Kor's engineers the shield specification that the Grays used. It would ensure that they traveled safely through the tear in space. Kor was willing to take all the help he could get in order to ensure the safety of his mates and crew.

The new shields also had the added bonus of providing them with total concealment from Earth's detection, which was something the Grays had demanded. Under no circumstances were the Arathians to make themselves known to the people of Earth since it would alter the Earther's knowledge of the universe.

The Grays had also explained that due to the wormhole's instability, ships could only travel in one direction through it. To get back to the original sector of space they would need to enter an alternate wormhole. That wormhole, however, was much more difficult to use because it was located only ten miles over Earth in the planet's troposphere, making it difficult to stay hidden from detection.

Besides having to worry about detection from Earther radar, the wormhole was also risky because if there were any Earther vehicles directly under the wormhole's entry point they would be pulled into the event horizon.

The Grays admitted that they had experienced a few such accidents over the years, some even recently, and had inadvertently pulled Earthers into the wake of their own ships. Thankfully, the Earthers did not understand the phenomenon and had given it the ridiculous name of the 'Bermuda Triangle'. They had created an entire superstition surrounding that area of sea in attempts to explain the strange events.

Kor didn't want to ask the Grays what had become of those unfortunate Earther vessels because nothing but the vast expanse of space waited for them at the other end of the wormhole. Assuming they made it that far. It was possible that the Grays had saved those individuals, but Kor wouldn't bet on it since the Grays wanted to be nothing but passive observers in Earth's development.

Kor didn't understand how the Grays could watch Earth for thousands of years and not interfere. They had watched silently as Earthers died from natural disasters, disease, famine, and watch as they destroyed themselves through war, religion, and greed.

Passively watching was not in the nature of an Arathian. For hundreds of years they had defended any species weaker than themselves from natural, or self-imposed, disasters. It went against all his instincts not to step in and help. He knew that even without Earth being linked to his species by DNA, he would still be en route to Earth to protect them from the Lazools.

Kor's primary concern was exactly how they were going to protect Earth with just the Adastra, which was a science vessel. They would be going up against a Lazool battlecruiser and, even with the enhanced shields the Grays had provided, he was worried about the safety of his crew, and especially his mates.

Thankfully Lacy seemed to be quite calm and after Ty had used the Med Unit to check on her after they arrived onboard, he found that she was just as healthy as before they attended the Galactic Council. Since then, Ty had finally stopped fretting over her health night and day and they were all settling into a routine.

Ambassador Rex had stayed behind to try to find a way to get the Galactic Council to ensure Earth's protection. So far he hadn't succeeded, however, he seemed determined to keep trying. He had assembled a team to go through all the historical documents available, in the hopes of finding a precedent for their cause, but so far to no avail.

"What's got you thinking so hard?" Lacy asked as she came out of the bathing chamber, looking delectably wet from her recent shower, wrapped in a towel. His little mate liked to shower at night and he loved how she smelled as they slept together.

Ty and Kor had agreed to delay love-making for a couple of weeks because they were nervous about the new pregnancy. Now Lacy was seven weeks along and, after his latest scan, Ty said that he thought it was safe. Of course Lacy had been protesting the entire time, claiming that it was perfectly normal for pregnant females on Earth to have sex throughout the pregnancy, but her mates had not yielded.

She wore outfits that she had replicated made entirely of lace, wore no panties, and had dropped her towel continuously over the past week in hopes of enticing them, but thankfully he and Ty had held out. Of course, Kor had resorted to stroking himself off in the shower to stay sane, but her safety and that of their child was paramount.

He was currently sitting on the large bench in front of the room's expansive windows. She came to his side and was immediately enfolded in his arms. She snuggled into his chest while he replied, "I was just thinking about what lies ahead for us."

She tilted her head to look up at his face. "Are you worried?" She asked.

"No." He lied, kissing her forehead and smoothing back her hair. "I just want to be prepared for anything, to ensure everyone's safety."

"Your own safety included right?" She asked.

"Of course." He said smiling. "But you, the baby, Ty, and the rest of my crew will always come first."

She frowned, but once again nestled her face into his chest. "Let's hope it doesn't come to that."

"Agreed." He said. "Now, I don't want to think about that unpleasantness any longer. I want to enjoy my mates, *thoroughly*."

He saw Ty's head perk up from where he was sitting, pouring over tablets at his console, and knew he had been listening intently. They were both starving for her after the long nights of abstinence, so when Kor lifted Lacy and carried her to the bed, Ty was right by his side.

Only a moment passed before he took her mouth in a tender kiss that quickly turned demanding. Kor felt like it had been so long since he'd enjoyed her delectable body and he wanted to rediscover her all over again.

He placed her down, gently, on the massive bed then began removing his clothes while Lacy watched intently. He didn't get far before Ty latched onto his mouth, his tongue demanding the access that Kor was happy to give. Kor reached up and grabbed the back of Ty's head to hold it steady for his demanding mouth as he took control of the kiss.

Ty's hands were on his shoulders pulling him closer to the heat of his body, but between them, Kor felt small hands working the fastenings on their flightsuits to free their suddenly hard cocks.

Lacy managed to get them both free as Kor and Ty continued to kiss hungrily. Kor faltered when he felt a warm, moist mouth dive on to his cock, nearly to his balls. He groaned, low in his throat, and reached down with his left hand to anchor his fingers in Lacy's silky hair as she began bobbing her head.

Kor released Ty's mouth and let his head fall back and closed his eyes to better enjoy the sensation as Ty latched to the tender part of his throat and began licking and sucking while his hands unfastened the rest of Kor's flightsuit. Kor reciprocated and began shoving at Ty's uniform with urgency.

Ty chuckled while reaching up and stilling Kor's fumbling hands. He made quick work of his own clothes but before he could kneel, Kor grabbed his hips and, instead, guided him to stand on the bed, next to Lacy, putting Ty's long cock right at eye level.

Kor moaned appreciatively and Ty's cock bobbed in eagerness. Lacy pulled off of Kor's cock for a moment

to look up at her mates and take in the
holding onto Ty's hip with his right hand
head with his left, he pulled Ty a half-step clo__
was then able to nuzzle his face into Ty's hairless groin.

At first, Kor ran his face over the tops of Ty's thighs, across his balls, and ran his lips up Ty's cock, stopping to give the tip a kiss before dipping back down and nuzzling his nose into Ty's balls again.

Ty was panting when Kor finally took one of the balls into his mouth and suckled on it before giving the other the same treatment. Ty threaded his fingers into Kor's hair and tried to direct his mouth to his aching cock but Kor refused to be led. He took his time, tonguing each sack and the area behind Ty's balls, until he couldn't withstand the suction of Lacy's mouth and was forced to pull her off or come down her throat.

Lacy wasn't fazed by the sudden pressure on her hair, but instead, decided to lie back on the bed and enjoy the view. She took her hand and slowly skimmed it down her body until she was parting the lips of her sex and showing her mates how wet she was for them.

They both stared at her in rapture until she finally told Kor, "Let me see you suck him."

Kor wasted no time and dove down Ty's cock like his life depended on it. Ty let out a guttural sound as Kor bobbed back up, swirled his tongue around Ty's tip, and then dove back down.

Lacy swirled a finger around her clit and watched intently at the most arousing sight she'd ever seen: Ty standing on the bed, his muscles taunt with unreleased tension, his hands in Kor's hair, while Kor sucked Ty to the back of his throat.

Without warning her climax crashed over her and she yelled out while pumping her fingers into her convulsing pussy. She looked up to see that both men had stopped to watch her come.

"By the Gods, that's a beautiful sight." Ty said with a smile, right before they both descended on her.

They laid on either side of her and each took a breast into their mouths. She had to remind them to be careful as she had been tender since the beginning of her pregnancy, but soon was begging them for 'more', and 'harder', when she couldn't stand their barely-there touches any longer.

She had just come a moment before, but felt like she'd combust if she didn't have one of her mates inside her. Since they were taking entirely too long for her liking, she pushed Kor onto his back and threw herself over him to straddle him.

She knew that he had allowed her to do it, so she rewarded him for giving up his dominance with an urgent kiss while rotating her hips along his cock. Ty moved behind her and fondled them both from behind until Kor couldn't take it anymore.

He lifted Lacy by her hips and Ty assisted by lining up Kor's cock with her pussy. Kor slammed her back down and they both cried out at the intense pleasure.

Lacy braced one hand on Kor's chest and reached back with the other for Ty, who was already rubbing his hard cock in the crevice of her ass, leaving behind his lubrication. He must have put a finger beside his cock because on her next downward stroke it went into her orifice and she moaned at the sensation and increased her rhythm.

Soon, Ty had three fingers inside of her and, other than the small amount of discomfort of that third finger on entry, she felt wonderfully full. Another climax was beginning to crest when his fingers were suddenly gone and she cried out at the emptiness.

Two strokes later there was something much larger

than the fingers at her ass and she experienced a moment of nervousness and stilled her movements on Kor's cock.

"It's ok, little Lacy." Ty said from behind while stroking his hands down her back. "I'm not going to hurt you, but I'm dying to have your ass. Will you try it for me? Please?"

How could she deny him anything?

She nodded and leaned forward laying fully onto Kor's chest. He tipped up his hips and kept up a slow and soft rhythm while Ty lined up his cock and slowly applied pressure. Quickly it became too much and Lacy was tempted to tell him to stop. There was no way she was going to be able to do this! It hurt!

"Push out Lacy, it will help." Came the advice from Ty. She did as she was told and he slid the rest of the way in.

"By the Gods, Lacy, your ass is heaven." Ty moaned at her back. She smiled weakly, pleased that he was happy with her, but wanting it to be over. The burn was intense.

They all stayed that way for a moment and allowed her to get accustomed to having both cocks in her at once. It hurt and she wanted them to finish so she wouldn't have to endure it anymore, but then Kor began to move inside her pussy and the pain was soon replaced with waves of pleasure.

Suddenly the pressure in her ass only added to the sensations, and when Ty started moving his hips in short shallow thrusts it felt unlike anything she'd ever experienced. She cried out, and couldn't stop her hips from trying to take their cocks harder and faster.

The men quickly got the idea and soon both were thrusting powerfully into her.

Lacy knew she wouldn't last much longer and knew she'd better warn the men but all she could manage to say was, "Kor. Ty. Oh my God… gonna come!"

That's all they needed. Both moaned and doubled their efforts and, within moments, she felt herself go over the cliff as she came on both of their cocks.

She heard twin yells as they both joined her, and then she collapsed on Kor's chest, nestled between the two sweating and heaving bodies.

Her mind was barely functioning and when someone reached down to grab the blanket and cover her, some time later, she hardly noticed.

Moments later she was gone. She was somewhere in the void of post-climatic sleep.

CHAPTER 10

Eight days later, Lacy stood beside her mates in Adastra's Command Center looking down at Earth. Looking at her planet made her heart ache, but she had accepted her new life, and that included protecting her former home. She, along with the Arathians, would do everything in their power to protect the Earthers. She smiled at herself for calling them *Earthers*.

"What's the Lazools' time to arrival?" Kor asked from her right.

Simdon answered from his station, "Two minutes until they emerge from the wormhole, captain."

"Put every station in high alert and make sure our new shields are at maximum." Kor ordered while his fingers flew over a console.

"Yes sir."

Kor and his mates had talked about the confrontation with the Lazools and decided that they would all stay in the Command Center together. Ty would leave to tend to the wounded when the time came, but he had an excellent medical staff that could handle the injured until then.

Lacy had flat-out refused to stay in their quarters and be 'left in the dark', as she had put it. The Command Center was closer to the center of the ship than their quarters were, so Kor preferred having her there as well. It was less likely that the Command Center would be compromised in a battle.

He didn't think that the battle with the Lazools would go smoothly. They had been trying, for a very long time, to get at Arath's resources, and Kor knew that they wouldn't let one science ship get in their way. The Adastra was no match for their battlecruisers, but he hoped that they could hold the Lazools off long enough for Arathian reinforcements to arrive.

"They're about to come through, captain." Simdon said from his console.

Kor checked the sensors on his own console and watched as the Lazool ship exited the wormhole and came into view. It was a massive ship with a cylindrical hull that had countless weapons mounted, in rings, around its circumference. He knew that those rings of weapons could move to track an enemy during battle, making it hard to get out of weapon range.

It also had forward and rear facing weapon ports along with a complement of about a hundred smaller fighter ships that could be launched during an attack. Kor admired the efficiency of the Lazools' design, and knew the Adastra was no match for it.

The most deadly part of the ship were the large ports that would open in the front of the cylinder and launch large, bomb-like projectiles. They would release the bombs into a planet's atmosphere, where the gravity would pull them down until they hit the surface.

The force of the impact would be enough to cause irrevocable damage to the planet, and kill all the inhabitants. If the Lazools released several of those bombs over the planet, Earth wouldn't stand a chance.

He heard Lacy's gasp, and from the corner of his eye saw Ty put his arm around their mate's shoulders. He didn't know if his little Lacy would ever be able to recover if her planet was destroyed, so Kor would have to make sure that that didn't happen.

"Incoming transmission." Simdon said.

"On the monitor."

The main vid-screen switched from showing the Lazool ship to showing its captain. Like the rest of his race, it had blue skin and a hairless, elongated head. It also had four arms, ending in three-fingered hands, and like the Arathians, they stood on two legs. They wore no clothes, showing instead an armored carapace.

The Lazool captain was the first to speak. "I see you've beaten us here. Your ship must be fast, although… it is not surprising, given how small it is. What do you Arathians use it for? Urgent deliveries?" It said, wheezing out the Lazool equivalent of a chuckle.

The insult was meant to ignite Kor's anger and to prompt a display of aggression that would start the battle, but Kor refused. He knew that the Lazools were members of the Galactic Council and, as such, the laws said that he was not allowed to attack them first. The laws *did* allow him to defend himself, but the race to attack first would be the one at fault, and removed from the council.

He would not let that happen to Arath, but he was hoping that, after the conflict, the Lazools would be found at fault and lose their status, leaving them highly vulnerable.

Since Earth had been denied membership, it was not protected as Arath was. It could be attacked and, from the council's point of view, it didn't matter. The Grays, however, added an interesting element to the entire situation, as they had laid claim to, and protected Earth, but it seemed like they weren't even going to bother showing up to watch what happened to their planet.

"Yes, that's exactly what this ship's purpose is, and I have a message for you from the Arathian Council." Kor moved around his console to be closer to the vid-screen. "Earth is hereby under the protection of Arath. Any aggressive acts will be seen as an act against Arath directly, and will be punished." He said in a calm but deadly voice.

The Lazool captain's face turned purple, showing a rise in temper, but Kor continued. "Leave this sector now because we will defend this planet."

The captain was so angry now that spittle was flying out of his mouth as he screeched, "How dare you, Arathian scum! We have already claimed his planet under Lazool law, and we will do with it as we wish! We will not be stopped by some insignificant Arathian ship!"

With that, the captain ended transmission and the vid-monitor once again showed the outside of the Lazool ship. There was a moment of calm before a beam lanced out from the battlecruiser, striking the Adastra and causing it to shudder.

Kor's fingers flew over his console making sure there was no damage to the ship. The new shielding the Grays had given them was holding. He turned to check on his mates, and Ty already had Lacy strapped into one of the seats.

Kor focused entirely on the enemy.

He maneuvered the Adastra to face the Lazool ship, head-on to present a smaller target, and fired back. The Lazools' shields held.

The Lazool continued to barrage the Adastra with hits while Kor did his best to evade, fire back, and issue commands. He tried to lead the Lazool on a chase away from Earth, but they caught on quickly and reversed course back to the planet. Kor knew that he needed to keep their attention for as long as possible so that they couldn't get into a position to release their projectiles.

Kor quickly caught up and maneuvered the ship around to impede the Lazools' advance on the planet. Suddenly, the Adastra lurched hard to one side and all the crew not strapped to something were flung to the right side of the Command Center. Kor heard a female scream a moment before he struck something hard and the world went black.

*****

Ty's chest hurt like hell, but a quick check showed nothing was severely injured or broken. He looked to Lacy's chair and saw that the harnesses had held. She was still conscious and trying desperately to unhook herself from the restraints. Ty looked left and saw that Kor had hit the wall several feel away and was now lying on the floor, unmoving.

Ty quickly unhooked himself and scrambled to Kor's side to check for a pulse. He put his fingers to Kor's throat and after a moment of fumbling, found the steady beat.

Lacy was, a moment later, his side running her hands all over their mate's body. She felt the other side of his head and her fingers came away covered in blood. She looked into Ty's eyes and saw his growing panic mirrored in her own.

"Captain!" One of his crew yelled from his left. "Multiple departments reporting damage, including to the enhanced shielding."

Ty looked up and said, "The captain is unconscious, you're in charge now Simdon."

He turned back to Kor, but was still horrified at what he saw. Thankfully, years of medical training kicked in and he quickly checked Kor's body, only to find that he was not breathing.

"Help me roll him over." He told Lacy while reaching for one of the emergency first-aid kits from under the nearest console. He pulled out the derma-generator and set it down beside them. The solution would encourage skin to grow and close a wound in seconds, but Kor's breathing was the real threat at the moment.

"First we need to get him breathing." Ty said to Lacy before placing his lips on Kor's and blowing into his lungs.

Lacy sat at her mate's side and watched Ty plug Kor's nose and breath for him. She had never been as scared, in her entire life, than she was at that moment. She had finally found a piece of joy and she was afraid that it was slipping away. She sat still, letting Ty work and, for the first time in many years, she prayed.

She prayed for the life of the male she loved, she prayed for the lives of the crew, and she prayed for the souls of every Earther on the planet below, because without the Adastra helping to protect them, their lives would very shortly end.

She realized her eyes had shut when she heard the glorious sound of coughing, and sharp intakes of breath, coming from the ground in front of her. She looked down to see Kor struggling for air while he tried to sit up and her heart soared.

Ty quickly took the derma-generator and held it to Kor's head to help stop the blood flow. Kor was demanding to sit up and get a damage report so Lacy had to force him back down, her hands on his chest, while Ty treated him.

After the wound was sealed, they helped Kor to his feet and got him over to his console.

"Report." He said while still coughing lightly.

Simdon answered, "The enhanced shielding took heavy damage. We've also lost all propulsion and weapons."

The crew of the Command Center all turned to Kor and awaited his instructions.

Ty knew that they all understood that the Adastra wouldn't be able to take another direct hit from the Lazools. Kor looked up at the vid-screen and they all saw the massive war ship maneuvering to face the Adastra head-on.

Kor feverishly looked over his controls and Ty could see him trying desperately to think of a brilliant plan to save them all, but as the seconds ticked by, and Kor's hands stilled, Ty knew that they had no options left and that these would be the last moments he'd have with his mates. The Lazools would fire one last round and the Adastra would break apart over Earth.

He looked to Lacy who stood at Kor's other side, with tears at her eyes, while she put a hand on her stomach. He could guess that her thoughts were with their unborn baby and the life that she or he would never get to live.

He knew that would be his biggest regret in all of this. He would not being able to see their little miracle born, or the joy on his mates' faces as they held their baby for the first time.

Ty looked at Kor, expecting to see his mate struggling to cope with the impending end, but was surprised when he saw Kor's eyes, wide with shock, staring at the vid-screen. A moment later, his fingers once again began flying over the console. Ty turned to look at the vid-screen as well and saw a very large, white ship.

That wasn't there a second ago, he thought.

Only a moment passed before the screen changed and the Grays' commander came onscreen.

"Captain of Lazool ship," the Grays' captain said, "you've caused quite enough problems for us for one day. Earth does not belong to the Lazool, it's ours, and we protect what is ours."

With that simple statement the screen once again showed the Grays' ship, hanging in space between the Lazools and the Adastra. Kor, Ty, and Lacy looked at each other in confusion but then saw a small white beam of light that speared out from somewhere on the Grays' ship.

For a second nothing happened, and then the screen lit up with a massive explosion.

After making sure that Lacy was alright, Ty looked up at the screen and saw that the Lazools' ship had been reduced to little more than glittering dust, floating in space. The Grays had destroyed an entire Lazool battlecruiser with a single shot!

"What the hell?" Lacy muttered from Kor's side.

"Indeed..." Kor said. A moment before a communication request was sent to the Adastra from the Grays' captain.

"Kor'ijak here."

"Is your crew alright, captain?" The captain asked.

"Yes, only minor injuries reported so far." Kor replied. "Thank you very much for your assistance. You saved the lives of my entire crew, my mates, and my child today. You have my eternal gratitude." Kor said, bowing deeply.

Ty and the entire Command Center crew also bowed.

"You're welcome." Was the captain's reply.

It was Lacy that spoke next, asking the question that was on everyone's minds, "Why did you end up helping us? The last time we spoke your people said that you didn't want to get involved."

"Earth is ours." The Grays' captain stated simply. "We protect what is ours. When we saw the threat the Lazools posed, and saw that your ship would be unable to defend the planet, we decided to intervene to protect Earth."

Lacy smiled at the captain. "Well, on behalf of the nearly seven billion people on the planet, thank you. I have to ask, what was with that weapon? I thought you guys didn't have offensive technology?"

The Grays' captain didn't seem to mind the question. "Of course we have weaponry. We do not like conflict, choosing instead to focus on our science, but unfortunately there will always be those to prey on the weak and we like to be prepared." The Gray captain turned to look at Kor. "How badly is your ship damaged?"

Kor checked his console. "We have no shields or propulsion, but life support is holding. My crews should be able to fix enough of the damage, so that we can move, within a few days."

The Grays' captain nodded. "Until then, we will remain in orbit and continue to shield your ship from the Earthers. Their technology may be primitive, but they can still detect us at this close of a range."

"We are grateful." Kor responded.

Lacy spoke up again, "While we're just sitting here, waiting for the repair crews to finish, how about you and I discuss a deal between the Arathians and the Grays, regarding Earth?"

She looked at the Grays' captain expectantly while he thought about her proposal.

"Yes, I think that would be an acceptable use of our time. We will contact you shortly to discuss arrangements." Then he ended communications.

Kor and Ty turned towards their mate who had a triumphant look on her face.

"I'll be damned." Kor said. "Ambassador Rex couldn't get the Grays to talk about cooperating with us and you managed it with one conversation."

Lacy didn't say anything, but turned and walked away with a massive smile on her face.

EPILOGUE

Lacy was being slowly lulled into complete relaxation by the sound of gentle waves and the shade provided by the nearby palm trees. She, Kor, and Ty were currently lounging on the white sand beach of a remote island in the Pacific Ocean enjoying some much-needed shore leave.

Kor and Ty had surprised her with this special treat. Ty had called it a picnic, but Lacy thought of it more like a honeymoon, especially after their near-death experience.

The Grays had allowed them this small token only because the island was uninhabited and they had taken a small shuttlecraft that was equipped with the Grays' special shielding to ensure that their visit went unnoticed. They were learning that the Grays could be very fair, and even accommodating, if approached with well thought-out logic.

The three mates had barely had any time to themselves during the past week, as Kor managed the crews that were working around the clock to repair the Adastra, Ty had tended the wounded, and Lacy had met, daily, with Captain Elom, the commander of the Grays' ship. They hadn't gotten far in their negotiations, but Lacy was still quite hopeful.

Earlier that day they had received a message from Rex, informing them that the Arathian Council had decided to reassign him, and that a ship would take him to Earth so that he could continue negotiations with the Grays. Hopefully, together, they would be able to find a way to take Earthers off-world.

Lacy was trying to not think about the hurdles ahead, and instead focused on the rare opportunity to be on her home planet.

After arriving on the small tropical island, the males had spread out a huge blanket that they piled high with all types of foods and drinks to enjoy after taking a swim in the warm ocean waters.

Lacy had delighted in her mates' reactions to her planet. Kor and Ty were dazzled by the blue ocean, the dark green vegetation, and the texture of the sand, but Kor had nearly killed a seagull when he thought that it was a predator stalking them, and Ty was convinced that the small fish near the shore of the ocean, were trying to eat his toes and other appendages. Lacy had rolled around with laughter as she explained that the seagulls and fish were harmless.

She couldn't imagine what kinds of creatures they had seen in their travels throughout the galaxy if gulls and small fish were what they were worried about, there on Earth.

She listened to the gentle and hypnotic rush of waves, letting the sun seep into her skin, but was brought back from the edges of sleep by Ty clearing his throat.

"Lacy, we have something for you." He said.

She used her palm to block out the brightness of the sun and saw that he had a small bundle of cloth in his hand. At first she thought it was another piece of clothing, like the dress that Kor had given her shortly after they had met, but once she sat up she saw that it was much too small.

She took the offered cloth from him and let it fall open. Something small and shiny fell out and landed on the blanket in front of her. Her heart soared as she picked up the small metal ring with a large, dark blue stone in the center, flanked by two light green stones that seemed to glow.

Her eyes began to tear as she looked up into her mates' faces.

"You said that you were going to miss not having a ring to symbolize our mating," Kor began, "so Ty and I thought it was important to recognize the Earther customs as well as Arathian. We researched rings of your culture and put a blue stone from Earth in the center and two green ones from Arath. Now it signifies both of our worlds, and the three of us united as mates."

Lacy didn't try to stop the tears from rolling down her cheeks. She loved those two men with her entire heart.

"Will you put it on for me?" She asked them.

Ty and Kor slid it over her finger together then gathered her into their arms. Locked between her two mates, Lacy knew there was nowhere in the universe she'd rather be.

THE END

ABOUT THE AUTHOR

Nicole was born and raised outside of Portland Oregon where she spent much of her childhood outside and at the beach. An artist at heart, she didn't discover her love for romance novels until college and since then has devoured hundreds. It was her husband, Aaron, that encouraged her to write her own.

She currently lives in Grand Forks, North Dakota with Aaron and their two beautiful and rambunctious daughters. They move often, but thankfully she can write from anywhere!

Nicole always loves to hear comments on her work so feel free to contact her at: nkrizek@gmail.com. You can also find her on Twitter or like her Facebook Page to stay updated on her newest projects!

Printed in Great Britain
by Amazon.co.uk, Ltd.,
Marston Gate.